THE PELLE ANCHOR CROSS

Richard G. Edwards

Cover Photo

The photograph on the front cover, taken by the author, is of the Harlan, Kentucky County Court House.

Acknowledgements

I asked my wife Carolyn and several friends to review the manuscript of this book.   They all graciously agreed, and I sincerely thank them for making the time and effort to do so. In addition to Carolyn Edwards, the reviewers were Mrs. Tracy Forester, Mr. Bill Green, Dr. Carl Peters, Dr. Gus Peters, and Mr. Jack Sterling.

Also, I would like to acknowledge my church, Anchor Baptist Church of Lexington, Kentucky. The symbol used by my church is the Anchor Cross, which inspired the titles of my novels and lead me to develop the story-line tracing the origin of the anchor crosses to gold blessed by my Lord Jesus Christ and later crafted into the anchor crosses by Constantine the Great around 325 A.D.

Finally, I would like to offer my sincere thanks to Kelly Elliott. She very expertly handled the layout of the manuscript and covers. Along with her husband Dr. Dan Elliott and children, Kelly recently moved to Italy and from there, through the miracle of the internet, accomplished the book's layout.

Dedication

I would like to dedicate this book to my family, both past and present. My past family consisted of my father, J.B. Edwards, and mother, Lillie Mae (Giles) Edwards. My parents were lifelong residents of Harlan, Kentucky. Dad was in the insurance business for many years, and then managed Mike's Drive-In at Loyal, Kentucky. He was a fixture at the Harlan Baptist Church. Many people in Harlan County knew my father. Even today when I return to Harlan friends often greet me as "J.B.'s boy". I love it! Growing up in Harlan I was constantly with my mother's family. Lots of "Giles" relatives lived there. My present family consists of my wife Carolyn, my two sons Giles and Kyle, and their families.   Carolyn and I were married in 1966. Giles came along in 1969 and Kyle in 1979. Giles and his wife Heidi have five wonderful children, Teagan, Jackson, Cooper, Clayton, and Lillie. They live in Eustis, Florida, and Carolyn and I enjoy our 3 month winter hiatus to Florida each year to spend time with them. Kyle and his new bride Julie live in Lexington, so we enjoy the other 9 months each year with them. The Lord has indeed greatly blessed Carolyn and me with a great family. That means everything!

Preface

My previous book, **The Anchor Cross**, was written in 2014. Many readers encouraged me to write this second book, **The Pelle Anchor Cross**. Lots of the same characters appear in both books, and the stories take place for the most part in the town where I lived for the first 18 years of my life, Harlan, Kentucky. I encourage my readers to contact me with comments. You may send these to richardglennedwards@gmail.com.

Should you desire a copy of my previous book, **The Anchor Cross**, you may either contact me at the above email address or order from any of the following:

www.BookLocker.com

www.Amazon.com

www.BarnesandNoble.com

May God Bless!

Richard G. "Dick" Edwards
Lexington, KY., 2015

Chapter 1

Harlan is a small town nestled in the Appalachian mountains of Southeastern Kentucky. The 1940 census showed Harlan with a population of 5,122, but has since dropped steadily to somewhere around 1,600. From early in the 20th century until the 1940's coal was king in Harlan. Since then the increase in automation used to mine coal along with the decreased demand has largely accounted for the sharp decrease in population in both Harlan and Harlan County. There is very little manufacturing and only small family farms. Government checks account for the bulk of the economy. But the people of Harlan are a proud and hearty lot. And justifiably so.

Creech Cafe is located on Central Street in downtown

Harlan. It is owned and operated by Fred Knapp. Fred decided upon graduation from Harlan High School to work for his father, who had founded Creech Cafe. That was 52 years ago. Fred, now 70 years old, is also the Mayor of Harlan, having decided 7 years ago to throw his hat in the ring to seek the mayoral office and he won in a landslide. He was then re-elected and continues to enjoy great popularity among the folks of Harlan. His cafe is truly a landmark. Kids from school come there to meet, greet, and eat daily after school. Old timers make a few hours at Creech Cafe a part of their daily ritual. Creech's has a large lunch counter, about a dozen booths, and a couple of dozen tables for patrons. There are two very unique features to Creech Cafe. Upon entering the front door, customers usually are immediately confronted by a large green Parrot that perches on a rod that Fred located beside the door. The Parrot's name is Polly, and Polly has a pretty good vocabulary. Polly is now about 22 years old, and she recognizes most of the regulars that come to Creech's daily, and often times greets them with "Polly want a cracker". She loves to mooch food from the customers, and would generally fly to any customer holding up a tidbit. The second unique feature of Creech Cafe is all the photographs and framed newspaper articles that Fred has put on the walls during his 52 year tenure. The walls are literally full of hundreds, if not thousands, of photographs and articles that Fred thought worthy of display in his establishment. Once placed on the wall, the photos and articles stay on the wall. Customers love to peruse these and reminisce about them with Fred. And Fred loves to tell the stories associated with them. He is known to spend hours with customers going into great detail about the person or event associated with any particular item of interest. Creech Cafe and Mayor Fred Knapp are truly both legendary in Harlan.

The Harlan County Courthouse and adjacent Harlan County Sheriff's Office are located directly across Central Street from Creech Cafe. The Sheriff's Office stands beside the Court House, and consists of 4 large rooms. The first room serves as the reception area and contains desks for two deputies. The next room is the Sheriff's Office, behind which are located two additional rooms, one being an evidence storage room and the other a small holding cell. Upon entering the reception room there is a counter, behind which deputy Rosie Cain can usually be found. Rosie serves mainly as clerk in the office, but occasionally is called upon to perform special assignments for the sheriff. In one corner of this room is a desk for the sheriff's principal deputy, Kyle Potter. Kyle has been a deputy for only about 6 months, having recently graduated from Eastern Kentucky University's Law Enforcement Program. Kyle replaced deputy Ape Cornett, who left to become an officer in the Kentucky State Police program. Simpson Brown is the only other deputy working the first shift, and he is normally out on patrol. Mousy Giles and Bill Black are deputies on the second shift, with Bill usually working in a patrol car and Mousy in the office. Because of budget constraints, the Sheriff's department is small. There is no third shift, and calls that come into the office during those hours are transferred to the Kentucky State Police. In addition to the 5 deputies in Harlan, the Sheriff has a satellite office in Cumberland, located about 25 miles Northeast of Harlan on highway 119. The Cumberland office has 5 deputies working out of it. So the Harlan County Sheriff's Office has a total of 10 deputies plus the Sheriff, J. Bert Sterling.

Sheriff J. Bert Sterling is 60 years old. He started as a deputy soon after graduating from Harlan High School, and has established himself as a very well respected officer of the law. Bert is tall and slender, and most think very handsome. He is hard working and constantly does his best to enforce the law in Harlan County. In addition, Bert is blessed with having a very pleasing personality, and gets along well with most of those he meets. After serving as a deputy for 15 years, he ran for the office of Sheriff and was easily elected. Every election since has been an easy win for J. Bert Sterling. He has now served continually as Sheriff for 27 years.

The Sheriff's office in Harlan has one additional, and very special, occupant. Preacher Puss is a 15 pound, gray tabby Cat that Rosie Cain had fallen in love with and adopted about 14 years ago. The cat got her unusual name when she was found by firefighters in the back room of a church building that had caught fire. Her screams were first heard, and the firefighters found her in a corner of a back room in the church that was filled with smoke but without flame. She was screaming at the top of her lungs, and after the firefighters had her checked out by a vet they tried to find her owner, but could not. The pastor at the church that burned said she did not belong to anyone he knew, and that he had not seen her before. He said she likely just slipped into the back room when the door was left open. So the firefighters brought the cat to the Sheriff's office, and when Rosie saw her and heard her story she immediately named her Preacher Puss, since she was found screaming in a church, and adopted her as a permanent resident in the Sheriff's office. A shelf was built for her beside and above the entrance door, and Preacher Puss loved to lay on the shelf and look out the window. She also expected her friends that entered the office to speak to her and give her a gentle stroke. Preacher Puss had gained quite a reputation in the office because of two instances that took place soon after her adoption. Those two events had to do with the fact that Preacher Puss has a strange peculiarity..... she hates guns! This was first discovered when the then deputy, Ape Cornett, pulled out his pistol to clean it the day after Preacher Puss arrived. The big cat leaped from her shelf above the deputy's desk onto the arm that held the gun. Claws were dug into the arm and the cat screamed loudly as the shocked deputy dropped the gun. Preacher

Puss then calmly jumped back on her shelf, laid down, closed her eyes and started swishing her tail. It was thus established that, for whatever reason, Preacher Puss did not like guns and everyone in the Sheriff's Office knew to not present a weapon in her presence. Then there were two instances shortly afterwards in which Preacher Puss attacked criminals that came into the office with drawn weapons. In these cases, when she saw the weapon she leaped from her shelf to the top of the criminal's head while digging her claws in and screaming at the top of her lungs. In both instances those attacked immediately dropped their guns. Preacher Puss's reputation grew throughout all the law enforcement ranks in Harlan County, where she currently is highly regarded.

Sheriff J. Bert Sterling had never married. He felt that his career demanded his constant attention, and although he frequently saw and dated Carolyn Potter, he remained single. Carolyn is the mother of Deputy Kyle Potter and works as a teller at the Harlan Miners Bank. She now lives in the small town of Wallins, about 10 miles South of Harlan, with her mother, who all refer to as Mawie. Until the events of about 12 years ago Carolyn lived with her husband and son Kyle in a small house only about a mile from Mawie's home. Carolyn's husband at that time was referred to by the nickname of Snake, and everyone knew that he got that nickname because he was indeed as mean as a snake. He was frequently drunk, and often times abusive to Carolyn and Kyle. He, along with 3 others, were arrested for attempted bank robbery and murder, and they all are currently in prison serving long terms. Shortly after this happened, Carolyn filed for divorce and was granted such by the court.

The events of 12 years ago that finally terminated in the failed bank robbery involved the then 10 year old Kyle (then called Kylie) finding a beautiful gold anchor cross while exploring deep in the woods around Wallins. This artifact had been carried into Harlan County in 1798 by Pastor Karl Seibert. Karl, and his wife Mary, were headed to what is now the town of Harlan to start a church, but were attacked and killed by Indians, and their covered wagon burned. It was in the remains of this burned wagon that Kyle found the golden anchor cross. After finding it, Kyle showed it to his mother Carolyn, and she suggested that they contact their pastor, Raymond Bell, to seek his advice. Raymond Bell is pastor of the New Hope Baptist Church in Harlan, and when he heard the story of Kyle's finding the cross he suggested contacting his long time friend in Lexington, Kentucky, Dr. Randy Peters. Dr. Peters is Director of the University of Kentucky's Center for Appalachian Research, and he has special expertise in the history of Harlan County. Dr. Peters drove to Harlan and met with Pastor Bell, Kyle, and Carolyn Potter and after hearing Kyle's story and examining the golden anchor cross agreed to do some research in an attempt to discover more information. His research uncovered astounding facts about the origin of the artifact.

The anchor cross found by Kyle Potter was about 6 inches tall, four inches wide, and about half an inch thick. It was made of pure gold. If sold for the value of the gold alone, it would be worth about $100,000. But the value of the cross vastly exceeded the value of its gold. In his research Dr. Peters had discovered entries in a diary written by Harlan County founder Samuel Howard, a friend of Reverend Karl Seibert, that described in detail the anchor cross found by Kyle Potter. Samuel Howard had met Rev. Seibert while the two of them were in Williamsburg, Virginia, and after

Samuel Howard and his family traveled to and founded the town of Harlan, then called Mount Pleasant, he wrote to Karl Seibert requesting that he come to Mount Pleasant to start a church. It was toward the end of his journey that Rev. Seibert and his wife Mary encountered Indians that killed the two of them and burned their covered wagon.

The diary of Samuel Howard had been donated to the University of Kentucky's Center for Appalachian Research, under the direction of Dr. Randy Peters. When Pastor Bell described the golden anchor cross to Dr. Peters he recalled reading about such an artifact in the Samuel Howard diary. In addition to giving dimensions and describing the shape of the anchor cross, Samuel Howard wrote in his diary that the anchor cross that his friend Karl Seibert had shown him had the words **Pax Tecum** inscribed on the horizontal arm of the cross. These words are Latin, and mean "peace be with you". The cross found by Kyle Potter had these exact words and dimensions. Indeed, this was the same anchor cross that was carried into Harlan County in 1798 by Reverend Seibert.

Also in his diary, Samuel Howard wrote that in his discussions with Reverend Seibert he learned that the cross had been passed down through the Seibert family for many generations. Karl Seibert was from a family of ministers. He also learned that Karl Seibert had been told many stories by his father and grandfather about mysterious occurrences encountered by those possessing the cross. Karl Seibert related one such story about himself, how while hiking in the hills around Williamsburg above the James River he had fallen through a crevice and as he fell the distance of about 100 yards the cross around his neck flew into his face and as he grabbed it with one hand the speed of his fall decreased greatly. It was as though gravity no longer existed! He then landed on his feet on sharp rocks beside the James River without being injured. He recalled that the cross in his hand felt very warm.

After reviewing these entries in the diary of Samuel Howard, Dr. Randy Peters began to trace the origin of Reverend Seibert's golden anchor cross. He found that the cross had been given to his great grandfather, Reverend Otto Seibert, by the Bishop of Munich, Germany. Apparently Otto Seibert had befriended the Bishop by performing an act that saved the Bishop's life, and in appreciation the Bishop gave Reverend Otto Seibert the golden anchor cross. Further research found that the Bishop of Munich had received the cross, for reasons unknown, from the then Pope Clement XI. And at this point in his research Dr. Peters determined that the cross had a name, it was called The Savior's Cross.

And there was not one, but a total of six Savior's Crosses. Constantine the Great, Emperor of Rome, after his conversion to Christianity, had decided to create the golden anchor crosses around 325 AD. In order to add special significance, he requested the gold from which to make them from Pope Sylvester I. Dr. Peters' research revealed that a number of gold bars, called Saint Peter's gold, were held by the Pope. These gold bars had originated during the time of Christ, and after receiving His blessing were passed to Saint Peter for use in establishing the church. Pope Sylvester I granted the request of Constantine, and gave him one bar of Saint Peter's gold. From this one bar Constantine was able to produce six of the beautiful golden Savior's Crosses. Constantine kept one cross and gave the other five to Pope Sylvester I. Dr. Peters was thus able to establish the origin of the anchor cross that was discovered in Harlan County. What happened to the anchor cross kept by Constantine and to the other four given to the church remains a mystery.

Chapter 2

Sheriff J. Bert Sterling and Deputy Kyle Potter walked into Creech Cafe for morning coffee. "Polly want a cracker, Polly want a cracker" greeted them from Polly, perched above the door.

"Forget it Polly, you're getting too fat," replied Sheriff Sterling as Deputy Potter reached up and gave Polly a gentle stroke.

"Polly sad, Polly sad," replied the bird.

"Yeah, and fat," Bert replied.

The Sheriff and Deputy proceeded to a vacant table toward the back next to the wall. Fred Knapp walked toward them with a carafe of coffee in one hand. "Morning boys," he greeted.

"Good morning Fred. We'd just like coffee if you please," said the Sheriff. Fred poured each a full cup after they turned over the cups setting upside down on their table.

Fred pulled up a chair and sat down with Bert and Kyle. "Everything peaceful in Harlan County this morning boys?" Fred asked.

"It really is, Fred," replied the Sheriff, "almost too quiet, if you know what I mean."

"Well, you just haven't recovered fully from all the action of 12 years ago," Fred joked. Then he pointed up to a photograph on the wall beside their table and said, "Ole Kyle here sure did look a lot different then."

"And he wasn't Kyle then Fred, he was Kylie!" the Sheriff responded. "Twelve years does make a difference!"

Kyle smiled as he looked at the photograph, and said, "I can't argue with you there, and I remember the day when that picture was taken like it was yesterday."

Kyle continued to look at the photograph and began to think about all the events that lead up to it. The photo showed Kyle, then a 10 year old kid, with a giant smile on his face holding a golden anchor cross in his right hand that was attached to a leather cord that held the cross as a necklace. The photo was taken during a news conference following an attempted bank robbery. During that attempted robbery Kyle was visiting at the bank where his mother worked as a teller. Four bank robbers, one of whom was Kyle's father Snake Potter, entered the bank in a plan to steal monies from safe deposit boxes owned by Harlan County's notorious drug dealer, Pretty Boy Maggard. The robbers had reason to believe that as much as 3.5 million dollars in cash was being held in Maggard's lock boxes. After successfully getting the bank president, Calvin Brown, to open the lock boxes the robbers placed the money in plastic bags and were ready to lock all the bank employees, including bank teller Carolyn Potter (Kyle's mother and Snake's wife), and Kyle into the safe deposit vault. Had this been accomplished, all would have died shortly from lack of oxygen. But just as one of the robbers was ready to turn the wheel on the vault to lock it, a very strange and still unexplained event occurred. Each of the robbers seemed to be electrocuted, and were rendered unconscious, falling to the floor. At the time this occurred, Sheriff Sterling was outside the bank getting ready to enter it to check on Carolyn. He was going to pick her up and take her home after she got off work, but she had not exited the bank at closing time. As the Sheriff walked toward the bank he saw a bolt of lightning apparently strike the bank out of the clear sky. Running inside the bank the Sheriff found the employees all tied up but otherwise unharmed, and all the bank robbers passed out. Kyle remembered that at that time he was wearing the anchor cross and it felt very warm. All the robbers were handed over to the Kentucky State Police, and the Sheriff scheduled a press conference for the following day to explain the attempted robbery. It was at this press conference that the picture, now on the wall at Creech Cafe, was taken by a reporter. At that same press conference the Sheriff announced that 3.5 million dollars in cash had been taken from safe deposit boxes that were owned by a criminal and that he was requesting the court to approve giving 1 million to the University of Kentucky Center for Appalachian Research for the purpose of building a room to display the golden anchor cross and tell it's Harlan County story (the cross was donated to the center by Kyle and his mother Carolyn), 1 million dollars would go to Harlan County for the purpose of building a monument and center in Harlan dedicated to explaining all the events surrounding Harlan's anchor cross story, and the remaining approximately 1.5 million dollars placed in trust for Kyle to be used in part for his education. His mother was the trustee. These requests were approved by the court almost immediately.

Kyle remembered how pleased Dr. Randy Peters was to have the golden anchor cross in the Center for Appalachian Research's new addition that had been constructed to display the cross and tell it's story. Kyle recalled how he and his mother had driven to Lexington with Sheriff Sterling and Pastor Bell for the dedication ceremony, and what a fine job Dr. Peters had done in his talk discussing his research related to the anchor cross. And all were equally pleased when the new monument was constructed and placed in a building erected on the grounds of the Harlan County Courthouse designed to inform the public about the events of 12 years ago. Kyle then remembered fondly his being able to pursue a college education at Eastern Kentucky State University in Richmond, Kentucky by using funds supplied through the trust. And he then thought how fortunate he and his mother were to have ample monies left in the trust for future needs. Indeed he had been blessed.

Kyle was brought out of his memory trance when Fred slapped him on his back and said, "Kyle, Harlan County will always be deeply in your debt for all your kindnesses associated with that anchor cross. At the tender age of only 22 you are already a Harlan legend!"

Kyle blushed and said, "Nice of you to say that Fred, but I only did what I thought was the proper thing to do."

Chapter 3

The Center for Appalachian Research is located on the campus of the University of Kentucky in Lexington. Dr. Randy Peters was named the Director of the Center about 20 years ago. Randy received his undergraduate degree in Sociology from the University of Kentucky, and then both Masters and Doctorate degrees in Anthropology from the University of Virginia. His major interest was in studying the history of Appalachian settlement, and after serving on the anthropology faculty at the University of Kentucky for about 5 years, he was appointed as the first and to date the only Director of the Center for Appalachian Research when the State of Kentucky approved funding for the Center in an attempt to focus attention on Eastern Kentucky hoping that such attention would result in new economic development for the area. Dr. Peters had a special interest in the history and development of Harlan County, and had researched such extensively. He had become good friends with Pastor Raymond Bell when Raymond lived with his wife Betty in Lexington prior to becoming Pastor at New Hope Baptist Church in Harlan. In fact, it was through Randy's sharing with Raymond his great interest and knowledge about Harlan that eventually brought Raymond and Betty to accept the call of New Hope Baptist Church.

Then the events of 12 years ago involving the discovery of the anchor cross in the ruins of Karl and Mary Seibert's covered wagon in Harlan County resulted in Randy's becoming closely involved in solving the mystery of the origin of the anchor cross. And finally with the botched bank robbery and subsequent awarding of one million dollars to Randy's Center for Appalachian Research he became more focused on the history of the anchor cross. After completion of the addition at the Center to display and describe the history of the anchor cross, a substantial amount of money remained that enabled Randy to continue his related research.

Randy was studying in his office when his secretary called him on the intercom to say he had a visitor.

"Stan Morton is here to see you, Dr. Peters," said Joyce, Randy's secretary, "he realizes he doesn't have an appointment but said he had something important he needed to talk with you about if you had a few minutes."

Randy knew Stan Morton well. Dr. Morton was on the anthropology faculty, and he and Randy had worked together on several projects. "Send him in," Randy replied, "I'll certainly make time to visit with Stan."

"Thank you so much for letting me barge in like this Randy," Stan said as he extended his hand to Randy.

Randy shook hands vigorously with Stan and said, "Always good to see you Stan. You know you are welcome in my office anytime. Please have a seat and lets talk."

Stan sat on the comfortable couch across from Randy's desk and said, "I just got back from a vacation trip to Italy yesterday, and I ran across something on that trip that I feel you will be most interested in."

"Italy is always fascinating," said Randy. "So much history, so many legends of history, and so many great places to see and visit there. What did you happen across that you thought would interest me?"

"Well, I flew into Rome, and then got a rental car and started driving North. After visiting Pisa, and checking out the legendary leaning tower, I traveled Northeast about 30 miles to the town of Prato, located in Tuscany," said Stan.

Randy replied, "Oh yes, I have been there. Prato has quite a history. Lots of great things to see there."

"Well, the thing I happened across there was in the Santa Maria delle Carceri. You familiar with it Randy?"

"I do remember the church. I visited it briefly when I toured Italy about 10 years ago. If I recall correctly the church was erected around 1500 AD, and is considered one of the earliest, most notable examples of use of the Greek cross plan in Renaissance architecture," replied Randy.

"I knew I couldn't stump you," laughed Stan. "You do indeed recall the church."

"But I don't recall any one thing in the church that was of particular interest to me, Stan," said Randy.

"You probably just didn't dig deep enough, so to speak," said Stan. "When I visited there I had a bit of extra time, so I ventured into several rooms located under the main floor.

I guess you could call them basement rooms, or catacombs. In one of these I came across a beautiful golden anchor cross displayed in a heavily protected case. The top of the case was a thick acrylic, and there were exterior lights shining through the acrylic to the cross inside."

"You do see lots of crosses in Italy," said Randy, "but not so many anchor crosses. I guess it reminded you of the one here in the Center."

Stan replied, "It not only reminded me of the one here, but it appeared to be an exact duplicate!! It even had the words *'pax tecum'* inscribed on its horizontal arm. Exactly like the one you have on display here!"

Randy looked like he had seen a ghost! "And it otherwise looked about the same size and design as our anchor cross?" he asked Stan.

"Identical, as far as I could tell," responded Stan.

"You are likely not aware, but my research determined that there were actually a total of six of the golden anchor crosses made by Constantine the Great from gold he received from Pope Sylvester I. Constantine kept one of the crosses and gave the other five to the Pope for the church to retain. The cross on display here at the Center is one of the five given to the church, but I have been unable to find out what eventually happened to the remaining four or to the one retained by Constantine. From your observation, it appears that the Prato Church may have one of these," said Randy.

"Were you unable to get any information on the other five anchor crosses?" asked Stan

Randy replied, "No, I have spent a lot of time and effort in trying to locate them. I have contacted both the Vatican and the Italian government with inquiries, but without luck. I was only able to establish where the anchor cross found in Harlan originated because we had a linkage going all the way from Pastor Karl Seibert back to his great grandfather in Munich, Germany, and from there back to Pope Sylvester I. There were records available that described Constantine's producing the anchor crosses from gold he received from Pope Sylvester I. But the disposition of the other 5 crosses remains unknown, at least as far as I've been able to trace. If the cross at Prato is in fact one of these 5 remaining crosses it would be the only one I've been able to locate aside from the one here in the Center."

"I think I can see a trip to Italy in your near future," said Stan.

"That would be a good bet," Randy replied. "A lot of mystery surrounds the cross here in the Center, and I would certainly like to not only establish if the Prato anchor cross is one of Constantine's six, but perhaps I might also be able to solve some of the mysteries surrounding the crosses by talking with someone at the Prato church familiar with it."

"Keep me posted on any progress," Stan said.

"You bet I will," replied Randy, "and I thank you so much for bringing this to my attention. I'll let you know what I find out."

As soon as Dr. Stan Morton left, Randy reached for his intercom and asked Joyce to check on a flight to Rome ASAP.

Chapter 4

Every town has its characters. Harlan is no exception. Richard Sanderson is one such character. Richard is in his mid thirties, very healthy and strong physically, but not so much so mentally. He roams the streets of Harlan dressed in various costumes. One day he may be dressed as Superman, the next day as Batman. Some days he dresses as a soldier. Recently he was seen dressed as a native American, complete with a feathered head dress and bow and arrow. He just enjoys being someone else. For the most part all this does not involve any law breaking, and most of the people of Harlan recognize Richard when they see him, and simply tend to ignore him.

Today Richard was dressed as a cowboy. He had a

cowboy hat, blue jeans, a cowboy shirt, cowboy boots, and a pair of toy six-guns holstered on his sides. He was walking around the court house, occasionally stopping anyone he encountered to ask them if they knew he was Roy Rogers. Most people just giggled. Some offered him a handout. Richard just smiled at them, and then walked on. He frequently encountered members of the Sheriff's department, and they too would usually just ignore him. Today he decided he would stage a "hold-up" in the Sheriff's Office. He walked up to the door of the office, pulled both "guns" out, and walked into the office as he shouted "stick em up". That was a mistake.

Preacher Puss was on her ledge above the door. When she saw Richard walk through the door with "guns" drawn she sprung into action, leaping down onto both of his outstretched arms with claws extended from all four legs and screaming at the top of her lungs. The claws dug deeply into Richard's arms, and as he felt the excruciating pain he dropped both toy guns to the floor and then shouted to Deputy Rosie Cain to please help him. Preacher Puss immediately released his grip on Richard when the guns hit the floor, and jumped over onto deputy Kyle Potter's desk and then back up onto his shelf above the front door. Rosie Cain was overcome with mixed emotions. She could not help but laugh at the antics of Preacher Puss, but was also sympathetic toward Richard. She knew the pain from Preacher Puss's claws was great, and she immediately shouted for Richard to sit in Deputy Potter's chair and ran to get the first-aid kit.

After "doctoring" Richard with antiseptic and band-aids, Rosie had everything under control. She scolded Richard for entering the Sheriff's Office, and after he had regained his composure she allowed him to leave. She then grabbed the bag of "Whisker Lickins" cat treats, and gave Preacher Puss several while she stroked his fur. Preacher Puss purred in appreciation.

Sheriff Sterling had been in his office during all the commotion. He had been on the telephone, and by the time he had finished his conversation and walked into the front office to see what was going on Richard had left. Rosie was laughing as she explained to Bert what had happened. Bert got a smile on his face and said, "That cat may be the best deputy in the State of Kentucky......and certainly the lowest paid!"

As Rosie and Bert were laughing about Preacher Puss's encounter with Richard, Mayor Fred Knapp walked into the office.

"I just saw Richard Sanderson walking across the court house lawn holding both of his arms gingerly, and they looked like they both were heavily bandaged. Something happen to him in here?" asked Fred.

Rosie explained again the encounter between Preacher Puss and Richard, and Fred joined in the laughter.

Sheriff Sterling said, "Mayor, what brings you to the Sheriff's office this fine day?"

"Got an important phone call I need to talk with you about," said Fred, and the two of them went into Bert's office and took a seat.

"You got my attention," the Sheriff said to Fred.

"Phone call was from the office of Kentucky's senior U.S. Senator, Rich McDonald. His appointments secretary was calling me wanting to know if the senator could come to Harlan to deliver a major address concerning a company that had announced to his office that they planned to open a new operation in Harlan that would provide employment for about 50 people. I told her of course he could, we would greatly welcome such a new operation. She said she could not disclose the name of the company or any of the particulars right now, but that the company wanted to have a ceremony on the court house lawn in about a month to make the announcement. I told her we would cooperate anyway possible, and that I would talk with you about the security that would likely be necessary. She seemed pleased, and said she would be back to me in a couple of days to discuss more particulars. You see any problem?"

Bert thought a moment and then said, "Biggest problem might be the mob of people there trying to get one of those 50 jobs. There's always concern when a U.S. Senator appears in public. Fred, you know the limited size of my office and also for the Harlan City Police. I would suggest you request from the Senator's staff that they ask the Kentucky State Police to take the lead in security for the event. They have lots more manpower than we do here in Harlan. My office will be glad to assist, but it would be best to have them in charge."

"Points well taken," Fred replied. "I'll make a list of requests and questions to pose to the Senator's secretary when she calls me. I'll keep you posted."

•••

Rich McDonald has been the senior United States Senator from Kentucky for 34 years. He had served in the U.S. Senate as both minority and majority leader. He was a highly regarded and respected politician on both sides of the aisle. He had the ear of the President, and frequently conferred with him on national matters. He also well represented Kentucky, and always had the best interest of the citizens of the Commonwealth in mind. He was now 77 years old, having first been elected to his office when he was 43 years old. Although reelections were always contested, and often times quite heated, he had easily won every one. Rich McDonald had the respect of his constituents in Kentucky.

He looked the part of a distinguished Senator. He was about 6 feet tall, slim, and with long, silver hair. He enjoyed good health, and had been married to his wife Sylvia for over 50 years.

Because of his seniority, Senator McDonald served on many committees. His most active committee work recently had been as Chairperson on the Appropriations

Sub Committee entitled "State, Foreign Operations, and Related Programs". His recent focus had been to investigate drastically cutting aid to foreign countries that had sheltered terrorist activities aimed at the U.S. and Western Europe. The Republic of the Sudan had been identified as one of the most active such countries. Senator McDonald's staff had prepared a recommendation that, if implemented, would result in cutting the majority of U.S. foreign aid to the Sudan. The Senator was currently reviewing this recommendation, and had plans to present it to his committee in the very near future.

Muhammad Ahmad worked as a researcher on the Washington, D.C. staff of Senator McDonald. Muhammad was a native of Sudan, but had lived in the U.S. for the past 10 years. He had become a U.S. citizen after graduating in political science from Georgetown University in Washington, D.C. He had been hired on Senator McDonald's staff because of his expertise in Sudanese government and politics. He had been a staff researcher now for almost 2 years.

Although Muhammad had gone through the usual background checks required for any new government employee, his activity prior to coming to the U.S. had been carefully "doctored" by Sudanese government officials to hide his work and support for 3 years with a government-backed terrorist group called the SPLA (Sudan Peoples Liberation Army), one of the most secretive terrorist groups in Sudan. Many millions of dollars in U.S. foreign aid to Sudan were diverted by the Sudanese government to the SPLA each year to support it's terrorist activities.

Although Muhammad had done his best to help conceal the fact that U.S. aid was going to the SPLA, the committee had been successful in establishing that this was in fact happening, and it's findings were contained in the paper recently submitted to Senator McDonald recommending the elimination of most foreign aid to Sudan. Ahmad had secretly and illegally reported the contents of this paper to the government of Sudan, and after meeting with SPLA leaders it was decided that Senator McDonald would have to be eliminated before he could present the paper and it's recommendations to his Appropriations committee.

Muhammad Ahmad was then told by the SPLA that he had been honored by Allah to serve as the suicide bomber to eliminate Senator Rich McDonald.

Chapter 5

About 10 miles South of Harlan off of Highway 119 is the town of Wallins, Ky. A mile or so before reaching Wallins there is a grocery store located on Highway 119 called Maggard's Grocery. The events of 12 years ago with the golden anchor cross involved this grocery store. At that time it was owned by Pretty Boy Maggard, who used the store as a front for his illegal activity, mostly to launder drug money. It was, in fact, his drug money that the bank robbers attempted to get from Harlan Miners Bank, some 3.5 million dollars. After the attempted robbery and exposure of the money, Pretty Boy and his accomplice Trigger Green left the county. Pretty Boy had not been seen for the past 12 years, but Trigger Green had returned about 6 months after leaving with Pretty Boy. The two had traveled to South America, and had joined with some friends they had met while serving in the Army together. These friends had established an illegal drug trade in Columbia and had kept in touch with Pretty Boy and Trigger.

Trigger had become home sick, and after a long conversation with Pretty Boy was told that he could go back to Wallins and operate the grocery store. Pretty Boy said he would sign the deed to the business over to Trigger. Trigger agreed, and had returned to Wallins and reopened the grocery store, retaining the name 'Maggard's Grocery'. Although the Sheriff tried to find evidence to tie Trigger to the illegal monies confiscated during the bank robbery, he could not. The lock boxes holding the cash were owned by Pretty Boy, and thus Trigger was in the clear.

After spending about a week cleaning and restocking the grocery store, Trigger made a trip to McDonalds in Harlan. Working the drive through window there was a fellow by the name of Fatso Chapel. Fatso had also previously worked for Pretty Boy by taking care of the grocery store. When Pretty Boy and Trigger left town, Fatso was left without a job and finally wound up at McDonalds. Fatso loved to tell jokes, and most everyone that encountered him had to listen to his corny jokes. Trigger went through the drive through and when Fatso saw him he got a shocked look on his face. Trigger said, "Hey Fatso, don't look so surprised! I'm back in town and reopening the grocery store. I'd love to have you come back and operate it for me. Pretty Boy is out of the picture, and I'm the new owner. What'd you say?"

Fatso said, " Hey Trigger, how do you stop an Elephant from charging?"

"You take away his credit cards," Trigger replied. "Surely you've got some new jokes after all this time Fatso!"

"An oldie but a goodie," replied Fatso. "I am getting a little tired of this McDonald job, when could I start?"

"How about tomorrow?" said Trigger.

"See you at Maggard's at 7:30 tomorrow morning," replied Fatso. "And thanks!"

Trigger pulled away from the drive-through window with his Big Mac, and was pleased to think that Fatso would be back with him the following day.

Since that time, Trigger and Fatso had made a living by selling a few groceries, but largely by illegal activities of one type or another organized by Trigger. The grocery store building was divided into two rooms, each 35 feet long by 25 feet deep. The front room, the one you walked into as you entered the store, served as the grocery store. The other room, the back room, was entered through a door in the middle of the back wall in the grocery store. The back room served as the office for Trigger, and it could only be entered when Fatso would press a button under the grocery store's checkout counter that opened the lock on the door to the back room. Also, the store had lots of security cameras mounted both outside and inside the store, and both Fatso and Trigger had monitors that allowed them to see what was in the camera's view.

The back room, Trigger's office, was very nicely equipped. In addition to Triggers desk and chairs it had state of the art equipment, including a computer, copy machine, fax machine, etc. There was also an inter-com that permitted Fatso and Trigger to talk privately. Trigger had not been able to get back into the drug laundering business. After Pretty Boy left town a drug dealer from Prestonsburg, Big Jim Owens, had taken over Pretty Boy's money laundering business. So Trigger was left with several small time illegal activities, including making book (gambling), credit card scams, telephone scams, auto theft, moonshine, and bootlegging. And he was always finding new ways to make an illegal buck. In addition, the grocery store "front" did bring in a few legit dollars. Sheriff Sterling was well aware that Trigger Green was operating illegal activities from Maggards, but with his limited staff he just could not get enough evidence to put Trigger out of business.

The lot that Maggard's Grocery sat on was in fact a 5 acre tract. The grocery store with parking in front occupied less than an acre. There was over 4 acres of vacant land beside the store. That land was what brought the visitor to Maggard's today.

He drove up in front of the store in a car he had rented after landing at Lexington's Blue Grass Field and then driven to Wallins, a three hour drive. As he walked in the store Fatso greeted him, "Hey there mister, can I help you with anything?"

"Looking for a Mister Green," the stranger said.

"And who might you be?" replied Fatso.

"Name is Jones," said the stranger.

"You got an appointment with Mr. Green?" said Fatso

"Just tell him Pretty Boy sent me," said Mr. Jones.

Fatso pressed the intercom button and said, "Hey Trigger, there's a Mr. Jones here to see you. He says Pretty Boy sent him."

"Send him in," replied Trigger, and Fatso pressed the lock release button and directed Mr. Jones through the door into Trigger's office.

Trigger, sitting behind his desk, opened the right top drawer on his desk to make available his 38 special. You couldn't be too careful he thought. Mr. Jones walked through the door, stuck out his hand to Trigger and said, "My real name is Anthony Beekins. It is a pleasure to meet you Mr. Green."

Trigger stood at his desk, reached across and shook hands with Mr. Beekins, and said "Fatso says you know Pretty Boy Maggard."

"May I have a seat?" asked Mr. Beekins

"Pardon my manners. By all means please have a seat," replied Trigger

When the two were seated Mr. Beekins continued, "I do not myself know Mr. Maggard, but I have associates who do. It was these associates that told me that Mr. Maggard had told them that he had given you this business, and that the business included not only the grocery store, but also had over 4 acres of land that was currently not being used."

"Something like that," replied a curious Trigger. "Please go on."

"Well, my business here has to do with that available land. I wish to represent myself as the owner of a company that would like to lease the 4 acres from you in order to erect a small factory that would be engaged in manufacturing computer related parts. The factory would employ approximately 50 persons. It would be my estimate that your land would accommodate both the factory building and enough space for parking. If we are able to reach an agreement I will compensate you $500,000."

"I'm a bit confused Mr. Beekins," Trigger replied.

"Please call me Tony," responded Mr. Beekins.

"Okay Tony," answered Trigger. "What's got me confused is you first said you wanted to represent yourself as the owner of a company.....not that you were the owner of a company. Secondly, you said you wanted to lease my land, but then you said you would pay me a flat $500,000.

I know that's a lot of money, but usually leases are paid per month....not a flat rate. Can you clarify these things for me?"

"You are a quick study, Mr. Green," said Tony

"Please call me Trigger....everyone does," Trigger replied.

"Well Trigger let me first say that I really have no intention at all of building anything on your property. And I am not the owner of a company that produces computer parts. Basically, I wish to put forth the story I just told you in exchange for paying you $500,000," said Tony.

"I see," said Trigger. "I am certainly interested in being able to accommodate you, and especially the $500,000. But just exactly what is it that makes your story worth $500,000 to me? I assume something illegal is likely to be going on, and I don't object to that.....just as long as I can be assured I won't get caught."

"Your sentiments are exactly those predicted by my associates after their discussion with Mr. Maggard in Columbia. He predicted your response exactly!" Tony replied. "I wish to use the story I just told you about the computer parts manufacturing plant in order to lure a certain person here to Harlan in order to eliminate him. As a matter of fact, I have already contacted the office of this person and told them the story I just told you, and they have tentatively agreed to this person's coming to Harlan to announce the new plant at a public meeting on the Harlan County Court House Lawn. So the $500,000 is yours for simply making my story legit."

"Couple more questions Tony," said Trigger. "Number one, who is this person you plan to knock off, and number two, my little operation here is pretty well known to Sheriff Sterling and his boys as being a bit of a front for illegal activity. Although they've never been able to pin anything on me, they still keep a close eye. So when you announce where this proposed plant is to be located, why wouldn't the Sheriff be really suspicious?"

"Let me answer the second question first," said Tony. "No matter what the Sheriff might think, the fact is that you do have the land here to accommodate our proposed plant. I can also assure you that my organization has taken all precautions to cover any checks the Sheriff might make to see if myself and the proposed plant are legit. My organization has as a part of it a current computer part manufacturing plant at a location in Mexico, and I am on record as the owner of that plant. So let the Sheriff check away, he won't find anything out of line. And we will apply for building permits with plans that have already been developed. I've got them in my car. There will be no reason for the Sheriff to think anything is out of line."

"And question number one?" asked Trigger.

"The answer to that will come only when you agree and accept the $500,000. It will be paid $250,000 cash today, and the remaining $250,000 at completion," Tony said.

"Best offer I've had in a while," said Trigger. "Lay it on me."

Tony opened his briefcase and laid out a package containing the cash. Trigger took it, quickly thumbing through it, and then held out his hand to shake with Tony.

"So who get's rubbed out?" asked Trigger

"Senator Rich McDonald," answered Tony

Trigger's face lost color. After about a minute he said, "You think you can do that?"

"Everything is all taken care of Trigger, he's as good as gone," replied Tony as he stood up to leave.

"One other thing," Tony said. "Don't even think about

double crossing me. My organization is large enough to take you out in a wink. I play straight with you.....you play straight with me, and we'll get along just fine."

"When is this activity going to take place?" asked Trigger.

"Soon," replied Tony. "I'll be back in touch shortly. I'm staying at the Holiday Inn Express in Harlan."

With that Tony walked out the door into the grocery store and headed for the front door. Fatso yelled at him, "Hey Mr. Jones, know what you call an elephant with a machine gun?"

"No, what," Tony replied.

"You call him SIR," said Fatso with a loud giggle.

"Have a good day," replied Tony as he left the store.

Chapter 6

Joyce, Dr. Randy Peters' secretary, had made Randy's plane reservations from Lexington to Rome, Italy. As do the vast majority of fliers out of Blue Grass Field in Lexington, Randy would be flying Delta to Atlanta and then from Atlanta to Rome. Joyce had then gotten him a car rental to drive from Rome to Prato. He had hotel reservations for one night in Rome at an airport hotel, and after recovery from the flight would then drive on to Prato where he had reservations at a hotel in the downtown area close to the Santa Maria delle Carceri, the church which housed the golden anchor cross that was the reason for the trip.

After driving to Prato, Randy located his hotel and checked in. After a brief nap, he had dinner at a nearby restaurant and then went to bed early in order to be well rested for his visit the following day to the church that housed the anchor cross.

Randy arrived at the church at 9 am the next morning. He followed the directions given to him by Stan Morton to the room in the basement of the church where the anchor cross was located. As soon as his eyes focused on the cross he knew his long trip had been well worth the time, effort, and expense. Indeed, the cross looked to be identical to the one in his Center in Lexington. After this initial visual inspection, Randy walked back to the main floor of the church and located the church office. Upon entering he was cheerfully greeted by a young lady behind a desk that asked if she might help him. She first asked in Italian, but then quickly switched to English when Randy did not initially respond. Her English was flawless.

"My name is Dr. Randy Peters," Randy replied, "and I am Director of the Center for Appalachian Research at the University of Kentucky in the US. I have a great interest in talking to the appropriate person here about the golden anchor cross located in room B3. Could you direct me to that person?"

The receptionist smiled brightly and said, "Of course Dr. Peters. The person you should see is Father Giovanni Territo. I believe Father Territo to be in his study. Please have a seat and I'll check to see if he might be available."

"Thank you very much," Randy replied as he took a seat in the reception area.

After about 10 minutes a door behind the receptionist opened and in walked an elderly priest who proceeded immediately to walk to Randy with extended hand and said in perfect English, "Good morning Dr. Peters, my name is Father Giovanni Territo. Everyone calls me Father Gi, and I would welcome your doing so."

Randy stood and shook hands with Father Territo and said, "I am so very pleased to meet you Father Gi, and I realize I have intruded without an appointment, and for that I apologize. But if you could share a few minutes to chat I promise to try and be brief. And please do call me Randy."

"No, No ..... not a problem Randy. You caught me early this morning, before I had any appointments or had gotten into any projects. I welcome your visit and look forward to trying to answer any questions you might have. Could we go to my study?" asked Father Gi.

"Just lead the way, Father," replied Randy.

"Thanks so much for your help," Randy said to the receptionist as they made their way through the door behind her.

"Certainly, Dr. Peters, pleased to be of assistance," she replied.

After walking down two halls the men entered the large room that was Father Gi's study, and he said, "Randy, please be seated. Can I get you coffee, juice, or anything?"

"No thanks Father, I just finished breakfast," Randy replied as he took a seat.

"I am told you are the Director of a Center at the University of Kentucky. You have traveled a long way, and I am most curious about your interest in the golden anchor cross in our basement. Frankly, the only thing I know about the University of Kentucky is that it has an excellent basketball team!" Father Gi said with a smile.

"Yes, we do indeed have quite a reputation for basketball Father," Randy responded, "but that has nothing to do with my trip here. A good friend and colleague had visited here recently and had noticed the golden anchor cross in your basement room B3. It particularly caught his attention because it looked identical to one that I have on display in my Center in Lexington. When he described it to me I knew immediately that I had to come here to see your cross and to find as much information about it as possible."

"I see," said Father Gi. "Well, you certainly came to the right place. As it turns out, I probably know as much as anyone about the cross, and I will gladly share my knowledge with you. But before we get too much into all the details, let me suggest that we include in our meeting the gentleman who actually owns that anchor cross. His name is Domenico Pelle, and he lives not far from here, between Prato and Florence. I feel that your story and interest in the cross would also be of great interest to him. I just had dinner with him a couple of days ago and think he is still at home. If you will allow, I will give him a call and see if he could come here to the church to meet with us. He could be here in about an hour if he is available."

"Oh, yes indeed. That would be very good," Randy replied. "So the cross does not belong to the church, but rather to Mr. Pelle?"

"That is correct," said Father Gi. "I'll wait to let Mr.

Pelle tell you the story, which I feel quite certain will be of great interest to you."

Randy replied, "Certainly, I look forward to our meeting"

Father Gi then said, "I will give Mr Pelle a call, and if he is available and can meet with us shortly I'll set up the meeting and then, if you would like, I can give you a tour of our church until he arrives."

Randy quickly agreed. Father Gi called Mr. Pelle and found him available and agreeable to meet in about an hour. Father Gi then took Randy on a tour of the church.

•••

Father Gi and Randy were intercepted by the receptionist to tell them that Mr. Pelle had arrived. When they got back to Father Gi's study Mr. Pelle was already seated there sipping a cup of coffee.

He stood and extended his hand first to Father Gi and said, "Father, so good to see you again, and I assume this young man to be Dr. Peters," as he shook hands with Randy.

Father Gi replied, "Dom, I appreciate greatly your coming on such short notice. Dr. Randy Peters here is Director of a Center at the University of Kentucky in the States, and amazingly has a golden anchor cross there that seems to be identical to your cross here at our church. Let's all have a seat and talk."

Domenico Pelle had a look of amazement on his face, and said, "Now you really have my interest! I had no idea there was another cross like mine. I am most interested to learn about your anchor cross, and without objection I'll let you tell us about your cross and then we'll tell you all we know about ours. May I call you Randy, and please do call me Dom."

Randy Replied, "By all means call me Randy, Dom, and I'll be glad to tell you what I know about my anchor cross."

With that, Randy told in great detail the story about the discovery of the Seibert anchor cross in Harlan County, and then told them about his research finding that there were six golden anchor crosses cast by Constantine the Great from gold he had received from Pope Sylvester I, and that the gold had been traced back to the time of Christ and had been blessed by him before presenting it to Saint Peter to assist with starting the church. After hearing Randy's story both Father Gi and Dom seemed stunned.

"I hardly know what to say," said Father Gi. "If what you say is true, then it is very likely that our cross is one of the six Savior's Crosses produced by Constantine the Great. And that it is made from gold blessed by our Lord Jesus Christ and passed down through the church. I think I need a large glass of water!"

"That is exactly what I believe," said Randy. "So Dom, could you explain to me a bit about the circumstances surrounding your anchor cross?"

Dom looked equally shaken by what he had just heard from Randy, and replied, "Randy, what you have just shared with us is astounding. And yes, I'll be happy to now share the history and knowledge that I have about our anchor cross."

"My great, great grandfather was Romano Pelle. He served on the staff of Pope Pius IX, and around 1865 the Pope apparently gave him the anchor cross that now resides here in this church. Try as I might, I have never been able to discover why he was given it. As I'm sure you are aware, Randy, the cross is pure gold and would be valued at more than $100,000 just for the gold alone. But in fact, it is priceless. The story you just told me about how the cross had been made by Constantine from gold blessed by Christ I had not previously heard. I knew only that the cross came from Pope Pius IX, and was given to my great, great grandfather Romano Pelle. After I received the cross from my father, Antonio Pelle, I decided to place it in the Santa Maria delle Carceri for safekeeping. I met with Father Gi and explained to him the value and history of the cross as I knew it, and asked if the church would consider accepting the cross. He agreed, but said they would like to display it. I agreed with certain stipulations. One, I wanted no description of the cross or its history on view, afraid that such information might lead to attempted theft. Two, I wanted only the surface of the cross to be visible in it's case, so that it's thickness could not be seen. This would keep anyone viewing the cross from knowing how much gold it contained. And lastly, I wanted the cross displayed in a very strong case with a simple light shining on the surface of the cross, and I wanted it to be located in the basement of the church, off the beaten path. Father Gi agreed to these conditions. So the few that ventured into basement room B3 could view the beauty of the golden anchor cross without knowing its history and value. It has been here now for about 20 years without incident."

Randy said, "My, my, Dom, that is fascinating. That pretty much pin points the history of your cross. A question I have is in regard to the unusual occurrences that have happened to those wearing the Seibert anchor cross. Are you aware of any such events associated with your cross?"

"I knew you were going to ask about that after you told me about the experiences you documented with your cross," replied Dom, "but actually as far as I know my cross was never worn as a necklace. As you are aware, there is a hole in the top of the vertical member of the cross that would permit it to be worn as a necklace, but as far as I know my family has always just kept the cross in a box. So if my cross possesses the capability for supernatural activity I am not aware of it."

"I understand," replied Randy.

"I think I can read your mind, Randy," said Dom. "You are wondering if the two crosses are identical not only in physical size and appearance, but also with the same abilities for supernatural control of events for those wearing them."

"My thoughts exactly," said Randy. "Just from looking at your cross in the display case it would certainly appear to be physically exactly like the Seibert Anchor Cross. But whether or not it is in fact made from the same gold and whether or not it possesses the supernatural properties I just don't know."

Father Gi asked, "If you had our cross in your Center to compare to yours do you think you might be able to determine conclusively that the two were made from the same mold and with the same gold?"

Randy replied, "Yes, I think I could. I could compare microscopic surface characteristics to determine if the two were cast in the same mold, and by performing tests on shavings from the crosses' sides we could establish if the metals were identical."

"Well, far be it for me to tell Dom what to do, but I think I would suggest that he consider allowing you to take the cross for examination. And if that happened, I would see no problem in allowing you to publish your results. But it might be best to not reveal the owner or location of our cross so that when it was returned here it could continue to be safely displayed in room B3. Your thoughts Dom?"

"I agree completely with what you say Father," Dom replied. "I would want our cross to be able to be properly identified, and I certainly would not want my identity or the location of the cross here in the church disclosed. Randy, would you consider transporting our cross to your Center for analysis?"

"I'm just totally amazed that you would allow me. I fully understand the value and importance of your cross to the two of you, and I assure you I would take every precaution to safeguard it at all times. In fact, with your permission I would like to wear the cross as a necklace under my shirt to assure it's safe passage to my Center," Randy replied.

"Airport security might be a problem," chuckled Dom.

"Well, I'd just have to take it off long enough to pass through X-Ray, but I don't think they could object, and certainly would not recognize what it was," said Randy.

"Then lets start to make plans along those lines," replied Dom. "And I'd like to suggest that the two of you come to my home for dinner this evening. We can not only finalize the plans for moving the cross, but I think I can provide you an Italian meal that you will enjoy."

Father Gi responded, "Sounds like a plan. Randy, if you would like to drive you could pick me up here in front of the church around 6 pm and I'll play navigator to Dom's home."

"Wonderful. I'll see you at 6 Father, and you Dom a short time later," Randy said, and the three stood, shook hands, and Randy departed, going back to his hotel.

Father Gi and Dom took seats again after Randy's departure. Father Gi looked at Dom and said, "My friend, perhaps I'm just being too cautious, but I feel I should share with you my thoughts."

"Please do," replied Dom.

Father Gi continued, "When we arose this morning neither of us had ever heard of Dr. Randy Peters. And now we are about to give him possession of a priceless artifact. Could we be making a mistake?"

"Father, we are on the same wavelength!" Dom replied. "That was one reason for my proposing the dinner this evening. I was planning on calling my Security firm as soon as I left your office to request them to do a thorough background check on Dr. Peters. By this evening we will know for sure his credentials."

"Ahh, I should never have had a worry. You are a cautious man Dom, and I appreciate that. I think we will both feel better when we get the report from your security firm. Perhaps you could give me a phone call after you get it, assuming that would be before Randy picks me up at 6 pm," said Father Gi

"Will do, Father," Dom replied as he stood and extended his hand to the Father. They shook hands, and Father Gi walked Dom out of his study.

Chapter 7

Sheriff J. Bert Sterling was talking with Deputy Rosie Cain in her office when the Sheriff's cell phone rang. "Sheriff Sterling here," Bert answered. "Sure thing, be over shortly."

Rosie said, "Bet that was Fred Knapp."

"Ladies intuition," Bert replied. "And, as usual, you are correct. It was the Mayor asking if I could drop over to talk about the upcoming visit of Senator McDonald. I guess he heard back from the Senator's office regarding the proposed event. Hey Kyle, want to accompany me?"

Deputy Kyle Potter replied, "Sure thing, I could use a cup of coffee. I'm getting a bit drowsy."

Bert and Kyle both spoke to Preacher Puss, and she returned a big meow, as they went out the front door and crossed over Central Street to Creech Cafe. Upon entering they noticed that Polly was visiting with a customer who was feeding her bits of food. The Sheriff and Deputy walked to a table toward the back of the room and sat down.

Mayor Fred Knapp walked up, poured coffee, sat at the table and said, "You boys want anything other than coffee?"

"I think coffee is fine for now, Fred," replied the Sheriff. What's new on the Senator's visit?"

Fred started, "Well, I got a call this morning from his appointments secretary telling me that things were getting firmed up on his Harlan visit. He plans to be here in about three weeks, on October 10th. I didn't see anything else scheduled for Harlan on that Saturday, so I told her I thought that date would work. She then told me that the Governor was also planning to attend along with his economic development secretary. I sort of had already figured that Governor Brad Shear and Economic Development Secretary Helen O'Malley would likely want to be seen at the event, since it apparently will announce new industry and new jobs. There's never a shortage of politicians willing to take credit for something good. Senator McDonald's office also told me that the Kentucky State Police had been assigned to take the lead on security for the event, and Post 10 here in Harlan would be responsible for all the security coordination. I was also told that the Governor's office had approved a budget of $5,000 to cover the expenses of erecting a stage upon which all the dignitaries and speakers would sit, a podium and sound system. Also they wanted us to publicize the event with one or more articles in the **Harlan Daily Enterprise**, with emphasis on the 50 new jobs that would be created. I've already met with the Harlan City Police regarding all this, but I told McDonald's people that I wanted your office, Bert, to be actively involved. I hope you'll be able to assist."

"Of course we will, Mayor," replied the Sheriff. "Fifty new jobs in Harlan deserves the attention of all public servants. I'll be in touch with the City and State Police, and we'll meet and determine who will do what and when."

"I knew I could count on you, Bert," Mayor Knapp replied. "Let's just pray now for good weather. Rain or a cold snap could cause problems, but typically our October weather here in Harlan is very nice."

Deputy Kyle Potter was listening to all this, but his attention had drifted to a photograph on the wall that showed a farmer kneeling beside a large pig with three legs. Kyle spoke to Fred and asked, "Mayor, that picture there on the wall of the guy squatting with a three-legged pig.... what's that all about?"

A big grin came across Mayor Knapp's face, and he said, "Well, Kyle, that picture was taken several years ago, but I recall the story like it was yesterday!"

The Sheriff replied, "Here it comes!"

Fred continued, "There was a traveling salesman driving through Harlan county. Now as you boys know, we don't have a whole lot of farming, but we do have some small farms around. The salesman was driving past one of these when he noticed the three-legged pig in a fenced-in area. His curiosity got the best of him, so he stopped his car and went to the door of the farmhouse and knocked. The farmer there in the picture came to the door and asked what he could do to help the salesman. The salesman explained that he noticed the three-legged pig and was just curious why it only had three legs. The farmer's face brightened up as he started to tell his story. He said that the pig was very, very special. He said that one time he was out working on his car, had it all jacked up and was under it and the jack slipped and pinned him down. He said he just knew he was dead. But then the ole pig came running up and got under the car and raised his back up and lifted the car to free him. The salesman responded by saying that indeed that was something, but how come the pig only has three legs? The farmer then said, well on another time one night in the wee hours of the morning a fire started in my little daughter's bedroom. That ole pig smelled the smoke and came running into the house, up the stairs, into my one year old daughter's bedroom and grabbed her by her night gown and carried her to safety......saved her life. To which the salesman again asked why the pig only had three legs. Well, said the farmer, after all that pig had done for me it just didn't seem right to eat him all at once."

Bert and Kyle started laughing so hard they jarred the table, spilling some of their coffee. Fred reached down with a towel and wiped up the spill, and refilled their cups.

"Mayor, that was a good story," Kyle said. "Wonder if that ole pig is still around?"

"Sort of doubt it, Kyle," Fred replied. "If he'd eat one leg then I bet the rest would soon follow!"

"I guess," said the Sheriff. "So, it sounds like everything is on track for the Senator's visit to Harlan on October 10th. I'll keep you posted on everything from my office, and you let me know any new developments that you find out."

"That I will," responded Fred. "Coffee's on the house..... you boys have a good day!"

Bert and Kyle thanked Fred, and then as they started out the door they heard, "You boys come back, you boys come back."

The two looked up at Polly on her perch and each gave her feathers a good stroke before they left.

•••

Senator Rich McDonald's appointments secretary was Sally Stevens. Sally had been on the Senator's staff for almost 15 years, and was highly reliable and trusted by the Senator. When Anthony Beekins phoned the Senator's office to make the request for the Senator to make an announcement in Harlan regarding the new plant and 50 new jobs, the phone call was transferred to Sally Stevens. She had listened to Mr. Beekins, and had then asked him a number of questions, including references. He had given her the Mexico plant as a reference, and she had called and talked with the acting manager there. Mr. Anthony Beekins seemed to be the real deal. So then Sally proceeded with the arrangements for the October 10th announcement in Harlan, including the call to Mayor Fred Knapp. Everything was on track.

Chapter 8

Anthony Beekins was quite well known in the world of international terrorism. He had grown up in Mexico City, and from an early age had gotten into the world of crime. As many like him had done in Mexico, he started in the drug trade. After several years he had made contacts with various terrorist organizations, and had left the drug world and established himself as a lone-wolf killer. He hired out to the highest bidder. He was intelligent, cunning, and reliable. After many years as a contract killer, his administrative skills became recognized and he in more recent years spent most of his time working for large, illegal organizations hiring him to orchestrate activities that would be of benefit to them. His visit to Harlan was one such contract, being hired by the Sudan People's Liberation Army, or SPLA.

Tony Beekins walked through the front door of Maggard's grocery. Fatso was stocking shelves as he entered, and when he saw him said, "If I recall, the name was Jones."

Beekins replied, "It was then, but now it's Anthony Beekins. My friends call me Tony, may I ask your name?"

"My name is Chapel, friends call me Fatso."

"Well, Fatso, it's good to see you again. I wonder if I might be able to see Mr. Green?"

Fatso walked over behind the check-out counter and talked into the intercom, "Hey Trigger, this Tony Beekins is here to see you again."

Trigger replied, "Send him in."

As Fatso reached down to press the button to unlock the door to Trigger's office he said, "Tony, Trigger said to come on in. You know what you call an elephant that never washes?"

Tony looked at Fatso and said, "No".

"You call him a smellyphant," replied Fatso with a chuckle.

Tony was shaking his head as he opened the door and walked into Trigger's office.

"Good to see you back in my humble establishment, Tony," Trigger said as he stood and shook hands. "Please have a seat, would you like coffee?"

"Please, Trigger … just black," said Tony.

After serving the coffee Trigger said, "Well, it would be my guess that you are back here today to give me a little additional information on what I have to do to qualify for my final $250,000 payment."

"Just wanted to give you a bit of an update," replied Tony. "I have been successful in negotiating with the Senator's office for a date for his appearance here. He will come to Harlan on Saturday, October 10, and will make a speech from the courthouse lawn. It is scheduled to begin at 11 am. That will be when the Senator's life will end. In the meantime, I have filed my documents and building plans with the County for getting a building permit to build on your vacant 4 acres. I have prepared a lease which I would like you to sign, and I will then submit it to the County Clerk to have it on record."

Tony then opened his briefcase, withdrew two copies of the lease, and passed them to Trigger for his signature.

After signing, Trigger said, "This sure seems like having to go to a lot of trouble for nothing since you and your proposed factory will be history on October 10th."

"Ahh," said Tony, "but so will be Senator McDonald. And my mission will be complete, and you will be $250,000 richer."

"So when you going to tell me a little more about how this hit's going to go down?" asked Trigger.

"I will only tell you what you need to know," replied Tony. "Right now the only additional item I wish to tell you is that a Mr. Max Robertson will be arriving in a few days, and will check in with you. Mr. Robertson will be presented as my plant manager. In fact, Mr. Robertson and I will both be on the stage when Senator McDonald makes the announcement on October 10th. The Senator will acknowledge me as the owner of the plant, and Mr. Robertson as the plant manager. Soon after that, Mr. Robertson will kill the Senator. You are to honor any requests that Mr. Robertson makes."

"I'll keep a lookout for him," responded Trigger.

"I knew I could count on you, Trigger," said Tony, as he stood and turned toward the door. "I'll be in contact."

As Tony walked through the grocery store Fatso was behind the checkout counter and shouted, "Come again Tony. You know what you call a man with an elephant on his head?"

Tony kept walking.

"You call him squashed," Fatso shouted with a laugh.

Tony slammed the door on his way out.

•••

Muhammad Ahmad had just received all his fake ID's from the SPLA. He noticed that his name was to be Max Robertson. Muhammad had also received quite a wardrobe from the SPLA. It included one specially tailored suit that had both the coat and pants fitted on the inside with pockets that contained explosives. He received three other suits that had similar pockets, but in these three the pockets were filled with enough cloth stuffing to make the suits fit similar to the one with the explosives. Among his instructions received from the SPLA, he was told that anytime he was in Harlan County appearing in public prior to October 10 he was to wear a suit with the stuffings.

This made him appear much heavier than he actually was, so that when he appeared with Anthony Beekins on the stage with Senator McDonald wearing the suit fitted with the explosives he would appear the same size to anyone who had previously seen him. He had also been given a prescription medicine that would have the effect of making his face puffy, so that his face would look more normal for a person appearing as heavy as he did while wearing his suits. He was to start taking this medicine one week before his trip to Harlan, which was now scheduled for October 1, 10 days prior to his rendezvous with the Senator.

His entire life had prepared him for the upcoming event of October 10. Muhammad was a devout Muslim, and wanted to follow the wishes of Allah. He had been told it was Allah's desire that he make the sacrifice, and that he would do. But he was apprehensive. Deep down he really did not wish to die But it was Allah's will. It would be done.

He felt confident he could pull the whole thing off. His English was sufficient. True, he did have a strong accent, but then his story was that he would be coming to Harlan as the new plant manager from the Mexican plant. He would say he was a native of South Africa, where he was educated, and then joined the Mexican plant about 5 years ago. Paperwork was all taken care of that would reflect his story. His education at Georgetown University and the 2 years spent on the Senator's staff in Washington had served well to indoctrinate him into the American way of life. When first told his mission he was concerned that because he had spent the 2 years on the Senator's staff he might be recognized either by the Senator or one of the staff accompanying him to Harlan. But he was told that none of the Washington staff would be traveling with the Senator, and that the Senator had only seen Muhammad a couple of times, and those were in staff meetings that included about 20 other people. In addition, the medicine's effect to make Muhammad's face puffy plus the padded suit would greatly alter his appearance. He also had a wig that he would be wearing which had streaks of grey in it to add years to his looks. It seemed everything was covered. He would leave for Harlan in about a week.

Chapter 9

Father Giovanni Territo's cell phone rang at about 5 pm. He was in his office.

"This is Dom, Father," said Domenico Pelle. "I just heard back from my security people on their background check on Dr. Randy Peters. Everything he told us about himself appears to check out. I think we can rest assured that he is who he claims to be."

"That is welcome, but not unexpected, news, Dom," Father Gi replied. "I just had a good feeling that with Dr. Randy Peters we were dealing with a quality person, but for something as valuable and important as our golden anchor cross it is certainly better to be safe than sorry."

"Right you are," Dom responded. "So we can now

enjoy our dinner this evening and feel free to continue with our plans for Dr. Peters to take the cross back to the U.S. for thorough testing. Are you still okay with all this Father?"

Father Gi replied, "Oh yes, I feel after hearing about the history of the Seibert Anchor Cross that we definitely need to get ours, which I will now start calling the Pelle Anchor Cross, checked out to see if it is truly one of the Savior's Crosses. And I would not know of another person on earth better qualified to make that determination than Randy Peters."

"I feel the same," replied Dom. "So, I'll look forward greatly to seeing you and Randy around 7 this evening. Do drive carefully."

"I'll tell Randy that. I'm navigating, he's driving, Dom," replied Father Gi. "Hopefully we will see you around 7."

•••

Romano Pelle had served on the Vatican staff for a total of about 40 years. The last 4 of those he served on the personal staff of Pope Pius IX. He retired from the Vatican in 1867. At that time he was only 58 years old, having begun his Vatican employment upon finishing school. He had found great favor with the Pope when only a few months after starting to serve him he discovered a plot that would have resulted in the Pope's death if executed. Having saved his life, the Pope rewarded Romano Pelle with one of the Savior's Crosses. Romano thought the cross was the most beautiful, and certainly the most valuable, of possessions. He kept the cross in the jewel encrusted case that it was in when the Pope gave it to him. He treasured and protected it with his life.

After retiring from the Vatican in 1867, Romano decided to purchase a farm close to Florence, and to raise grapes that hopefully would prove satisfactory for making wine. He was successful beyond his wildest dreams. In about 20 years the Pelle vineyard and winery was established as one of Italy's finest. Generations of Pelles followed in Romano's footsteps, and each added greatly to the success of the family business. Domenico Pelle was the current owner, and he looked forward to passing the business to his sons in the not too distant future.

And the golden anchor cross had also been passed down through the generations. It was not long after Dom's father, Antonio Pelle, passed the cross to his son that Dom decided to place it with Father Gi in the Santa Maria delle Carceri. That was about 20 years ago.

Under Dom's guidance, the Pelle winery continued to flourish and expand. Pelle wines started to be exported to many new clients throughout the world. Business had never been better.

•••

Randy tooted his horn as he drove up in front of the church. Father Gi was standing at the top of the church steps reading a newspaper. When he heard the horn he dropped the newspaper and with a nod and a smile acknowledged Randy's arrival and started down the steps.

As he opened the passenger side door to get in Father Gi said, "Good evening Dr. Peters, you are right on time, exactly 6 pm."

Randy replied, "I started to get hungry about an hour ago, so I certainly didn't want to be late! Good to see you again Father Gi."

Randy pulled away from the church and headed into the Tuscany countryside.

"I think I should warn you about Dom's domicile," Father Gi commented. "You need to be aware that he is a very, very wealthy gentleman. He operates a vineyard and winery that go back to his great, great grandfather. Pelle wines are among the best in Italy, and have now also established a superb world-wide reputation and distribution."

"So I guess we won't be having Pizza and beer for dinner, huh!" replied Randy.

"I think that's a safe bet," answered Father Gi. "Dom has a whole army of chefs, and it would be my bet that he has challenged one or more of them to come up with a superb dinner for us this evening."

"My gastric juices are flowing even more, Father," replied Randy. "I had sort of figured that anyone owning one of the Savior's Crosses might well be worth some money, but your description far exceeds my expectations."

"But let me hasten to say," Father Gi replied, "that while Dom is certainly worth mega bucks, to use an American phrase, he is also a very quality person. I have known him well for over 20 years, and have certainly come to greatly respect him as a person, irrespective of his wealth. If he were homeless, he would still be my good friend."

Randy grinned and said, "I know exactly what you mean, Father. I could detect even in the short time I had with the two of you that there was great mutual respect. If you would permit me to say, I think each of you have been greatly blessed by knowing the other."

"What a kind thing to say," said the Father. "I think you are right. I know that I feel tremendously blessed to count Dom among my friends."

After about 40 minutes of driving from Prato toward Florence Father Gi said, "Starting right here if you will notice there are vineyards on both sides of the road. For as far as you can see these are Pele vineyards. We'll be at the entrance to Dom's residence in about 5 minutes. It will be on your left."

No missing it. The entrance and gates likely cost far more than my home, thought Randy. He drove up to the gate. There was a guard house there, and a young man dressed in a suit walked from it to the car, and said, "You must be Dr. Peters. I recognize Father Gi."

Randy responded, "I am, and you have correctly identified the Father!"

To which the guard smiled and said, "Mr. Pelle is

expecting you. Please just proceed up the driveway and park in the lot in front of the house."

"Thank you Sir," responded Randy and he followed the directions.

"Father, this is truly a magnificent home! We have a lot of large, lovely homes in and around Lexington, but I can't remember seeing one more beautiful than this. I wonder how old it is?"

"Dom tells me that his grandfather built the home. It's about 100 years old. And Randy, that's not really old for homes here in Italy!" replied Father Gi. "But I'll certainly agree with you that it is grand. I get lost in it on almost every visit!"

The two walked to the door and pressed the bell button. It was quickly answered by an elderly lady dressed in a maid's uniform. She presented the gentlemen with a big smile, and said, "Father Gi, so very good to see you again, and I understand this gentleman is Dr. Peters. Welcome to the Pelle home. Mr. Pelle is anxiously awaiting you in his study. Please follow me."

"Thank you Sabrina, good to see you again. We shall follow," said Father Gi.

Sabrina led them through two long hallways, each with magnificent paintings hung on the walls, and then into the Dom's study. He was just hanging up the phone when they arrived. He walked from behind his desk and shook hands with Randy and Father Gi, and said, "Gentlemen, welcome to my humble home."

Randy burst out laughing, and Father Gi got a large smile on his face.

"Dom, humble is hardly a word to associate with this grand home and grounds!" Randy replied. "It is truly lovely beyond words. Thank you so very much for inviting me to dinner and to visit you here."

"My pleasure indeed," said Dom. I apologize that my wife and sons are on a trip to Milan. I do wish they could have been here. Please, please be seated and lets chat. But do allow me to offer you a glass of wine. I do think I could probably find something suitable."

Randy and Father Gi both chuckled and agreed with big smiles.

Sabrina materialized with what was undoubtedly glasses of fine Pelle wine for everyone.

Dom began, "Gentlemen I just hung up the phone

talking with my arrangements secretary. I told her to please rearrange my appointments for the next month."

Father Gi responded, "Going somewhere Dom?"

"I hope it is not too presumptuous on my part, but I have made the decision that I would like to accompany Randy back to the U.S. to visit his Center and to tour a bit around the central part of the country. I have visited America many times, but always on either the East or West coast. I have not had a chance to visit mid America. I'm told Kentucky is quite lovely, and in addition to visiting Randy's Center and seeing the Seibert Anchor Cross I would love to tour the state a bit. Am I being too forward, Randy?"

"Indeed you are not, my friend," Randy replied. "I think that is a splendid idea. Although my home in Lexington is nowhere in the class of your lovely home, I would insist that you stay with me. I do have plenty of room, and I would count it as an honor to host you."

Dom replied, "Then it will be so. I will look forward greatly to my trip with you. May I ask when you plan to return?"

Randy said, "Frankly, the sole reason for my visit here

was to view your anchor cross. That has been accomplished. If it works for you we could return as early as tomorrow."

"Ahh, I was hoping you would say that," replied Dom. "I took the liberty to request my arrangements secretary to book the two of us on a flight leaving Rome at noon tomorrow. And I hope you won't object to first class seats!"

"What a treat that will be for a University employee!" said Randy. "We are normally required to travel economy. Sitting up front will be a big blessing. Thank you so much for your generosity, Dom."

Dom replied, "If you could return your rental car in Prato I'll plan to pick you up at your hotel around 8 tomorrow morning and we'll drive to Rome for our flight."

"Yes, there's an office for the rental next door to my hotel, I can drop off the car when I get back there this evening and be all set to ride with you tomorrow. Thanks again!" replied Randy.

"So," Dom said, "now that that's taken care of, lets talk a bit about the Pelle Anchor Cross. After you left the church yesterday, Randy, Father Gi and I walked down to the basement room B3. There are two keys to the case displaying the Pelle Anchor Cross. I have one and Father Gi has one. I asked Father Gi if he would please open the case, that I wanted to remove the anchor cross to take with me back to my home in anticipation that you would be transporting it to the U.S. He did, and I have it here in my desk."

Dom opened a desk drawer, and withdrew the beautiful golden Pelle anchor cross. He handed it to Randy.

Randy's eyes opened wide, and his hands started to shake slightly as he held the artifact. "As much as I've held and studied the Seibert Anchor Cross at my Center, I'm still in total awe looking upon this treasure. It is beautiful beyond description. And I see you've added a leather necklace to allow me to wear the cross on the trip back home!"

"I thought that would be a good idea, Randy," Dom replied. "I could not think of a safer way to transport it."

Father Gi said, "If you would permit me, I would like one last touch before the trip."

Randy said, "Absolutely, Father."

Randy handed the cross to Father Gi. Father Gi held it directly in front of his eyes and slowly turned the cross

360 degrees, absorbing it's radiance and beauty. He finally said, "Thank you, I feel like I'm saying good-bye to a friend getting ready to take a trip!" He then handed the cross back to Randy.

"If I may, I'll just hang it around my neck now, and tuck it under my shirt."

"Sounds good to me. Now I think it's time for dinner. Try and not spill anything on your chest, Randy," Dom said with a smile and chuckle.

Randy and Father Gi followed Dom as they walked to the dining room.

Chapter 10

Mayor Knapp, Sheriff Sterling, and Deputy Potter were all seated at a table in Creech Cafe enjoying morning coffee and swapping tales.

The Mayor got down to business and said, "Boys, the governor's economic development people have been driving me crazy. Ever since they learned that Senator McDonald was going to come here to make the announcement about that new plant with 50 new jobs they've been trying every way they can think of to get more interest stirred up, and publicity for the governor and their office I'm sure."

"Well, that's about what you would expect from political types," commented the Sheriff, "and I guess the truth is it wouldn't hurt to have a big crowd here for it. As bad as unemployment is in Harlan, you'd think that announcing 50 new jobs would be met with lots of interest, but anything to draw more attention to it would be good."

"I guess," Fred replied. "What they came up with was an attempt to try and leverage on the publicity that we got 12 years ago by asking me to try and arrange with Dr. Randy Peters to bring the Seibert Anchor Cross here for display at the announcement. I told them I really didn't think that would be appropriate, but they insisted. I tried calling Randy and his office told me he was out of the country, on a trip to Italy, but they expected him back in the next few days. He's going to give me a call then, but I don't know if he'll go along with the idea. What'd you guys think?"

Deputy Kyle Potter said, "I think it's a good idea. Most everyone in Harlan County knows the story about that Seibert Anchor Cross, and to get a chance to actually see it would certainly generate a lot of interest. If Randy would go along with it I think it would result in one huge crowd for the announcement. Bert, what's your thoughts about it?"

The Sheriff responded, "No doubt it would attract a lot of people. The problem I see is one of security. To know that a priceless artifact was going to be on stage that day could draw trouble. But then we're supposed to have plenty of troopers from the Kentucky State Police to help with security. I think we could handle it, but it would certainly put a different light on things. Of course if Randy doesn't allow it, then it's a moot point anyway. I would suggest we just wait until you hear from him, Fred, and then start making plans accordingly."

"Good comments fellows," Fred responded. "That's just what I'll do. When Randy gets back with me I'll let you know, and we can go from there."

Just then a lady walked up to the table where Fred, Bert, and Kyle were seated and said, "Mayor, when I was in here last week I noticed the picture stuck on the wall there beside your table. It's a picture of two really mean looking men and I just had to come over to get you to tell me what it's all about. I hope I'm not interfering with any official business here."

"Not at all, Mabel," responded the Mayor as he stood and greeted her. "As you know, I'm always happy to talk about my wall hangings! And you are certainly right, those two are about as mean as any two men that ever walked in Harlan County."

The Sheriff punched the Deputy with a wink.

Fred continued, "Those two men were the Blackburn brothers, Bad Bob and Bubba. They lived near Evarts, about 10 miles from here. The picture was taken maybe 25 years ago, just before Bad Bob got into some serious trouble. When the Kentucky State Police got a tip that Bad Bob was involved in some kind of illegal activity they went to his home to talk and a big fight broke out. Bad Bob made the mistake of drawing a gun on one of the troopers. I think that got him shot about 4 times. Before the funeral, which was attended by very few people .... Bad Bob just didn't have friends, his brother Bubba apparently started to feel sorry for Bad Bob and his reputation, so he decided he would offer $1,000 to any preacher who would preach the funeral and during the course of the funeral declare Bad Bob a saint. After contacting several preachers without any luck, he finally found one that apparently really needed the money for his church, and told Bubba he would do it. He would preach the funeral and he would declare Bad Bob Blackburn a saint. This really pleased Bubba, so he paid the preacher the $1,000. On the day of the funeral, the preacher stood up and conducted the service. At the very end he said, 'As everyone here well knows, Bad Bob Blackburn was not a perfect man. But compared to his brother, Bubba, he was a saint!' I think that preacher is probably still running to get away from Bubba."

Mabel giggled, and said, "Mayor, you do have the best stories!!" And she turned and left.

Bert said, "Fred, when I look around this room and see all these thousands of pictures and articles on the walls I find it simply amazing that you can remember all the stories associated with each one. But you do, and I must say that you do a great job of telling about them."

Fred responded, "Well thank you Sheriff, it's kind of my hobby. I do enjoy it."

The three stood, and as Fred walked with Bert and Kyle toward the door he said, "I'll keep you posted on things regarding the October 10th announcement by Senator McDonald. You boys have a good day."

The Sheriff and Deputy walked back to their offices.

Chapter 11

Randy had checked out of his hotel, and was waiting just outside for Dom Pelle to pick him up for their ride to the Rome airport. Randy was running a bit ahead of the scheduled 8 am pick up time, and had seated himself on a bench in front of the hotel. As he sat he thought back to the events of last evening. He felt so good to have met Father Gi and Dom Pelle, things just could not have gone better. His visit with Dom in his magnificent estate will never be forgotten. And the meal was the finishing touch! Never, ever had he enjoyed a meal more than the one last evening. Although the food was superb, it was the total ambiance that made it incredible. The dining room itself was large enough to seat an army, the paintings that graced the walls were obviously original oils of great value, the dining table had been passed down through Pelle generations, the table covering was exquisite, and the dinner ware was sterling as beautiful as he had encountered. Two chefs had marched into the dining room to announce and describe in great detail the food that was to follow. House staff then presented each course of the meal with great flair. And the wine, the Pelle wine, was delightful. Truly a meal to be long remembered.

"You ready to roll," Dom shouted from his car.

Randy jerked his head toward the voice and said, "Yes sir, I surely am. I was just daydreaming about the wonderful evening we had."

Randy stood, grabbed his suitcase and placed it in the trunk after Dom hit the release button, and then seated himself in the passenger seat. Off they started for Rome.

"Dom, I just cannot begin to tell you how much I enjoyed last evening. The meal was just the finest I have ever had, and your home is something that I'll be talking about for some time to come," Randy said.

"It was a most enjoyable evening," replied Dom. "I've appreciated and highly regarded Father Gi for many years, and always enjoy spending time with him. And I feel now that he has brought me a great new friend."

Randy said, "Well, thank you, and likewise I feel that I have found 2 great new friends. As outstanding as the meal and seeing your beautiful home were, I especially enjoyed the discussions we had. Father Gi can certainly spin tales with the best of them, and the stories you regaled us with about your ancestors and the development of the Pelle vineyard and winery were highlights of my trip."

Dom looked over and appeared to examine Randy closely, and then said, "I was looking to see if I could tell you were wearing the Pelle Anchor Cross, but I can't tell."

"Yeah, I sort of dressed so as to hide it," Randy replied. "I placed the cross outside my shirt, but then wore this sweater over it. Then by wearing my sport coat I can further hide the bulge from the cross. When we get to the airport and have to go through security I thought if you were behind me it would help to keep other people from seeing it when I take it off to put in the tray to pass through X-ray. Also, I plan to place a magazine I'll be carrying over the cross so that the security people will be less likely to see it. On X-ray it'll just show up as a metal cross, and I'm sure the security people see a lot of those, so likely they won't need to inspect it."

"Sounds like a plan to me," replied Dom. "I think it should get through without incident."

Randy and Dom continued their trip with pleasant conversation. They arrived at the airport about 90 minutes ahead of their plane's departure time. Dom got his car parked, and the two walked into the terminal. The plan to get the Pelle Anchor Cross through security went exactly as envisioned. The security people seemed not the least curious seeing the anchor cross pop up on their X-ray screen, and they did not notice as Randy replaced the cross necklace around his neck and placed the cross back under his sweater. They then walked to the departure gate and took seats to await the call to board their plane.

Being in first class, they were the first to board. After getting in and settled Randy commented, "Dom, I could get used to traveling like this! Large, padded, reclining seats. Television, champagne, waited on head to toe .... thanks again for allowing me to accompany you in such luxury."

"Glad to be able to," Dom replied.

The door going into the cockpit was still open and

Randy could see the pilot and co-pilot running their checklist. Passengers flooded into both aisles of the plane as they located their seats. Finally, all were aboard, the door to the cockpit was closed and locked, and the plane pushed off. As Randy had done on his trip to Rome, they were flying Delta, and bound for Atlanta. After a stop there for about 1 hour they would board their final flight to Lexington. The plane taxied to the runway, and they were next for departure!

The Captain was Donald Schrodt. Captain Schrodt was 63 years old, a bit overweight, but otherwise in good health as far as he knew. He had been flying with Delta for just over 20 years, and was looking forward to a nice retirement in the not too distant future. He loved to fly fish for trout, and hoped his retirement would allow him ample time to pursue his fishing. The co-pilot was 55 year old Sam Heard. He had also been flying with Delta for a bit over 20 years and was looking forward greatly to getting his fourth stripe and the accompanying raise and benefits of a captain. That would likely happen later this year. Sam was also generally in good health, but had been having some chest pains lately. He didn't want to put up any kind of flag that would cause a problem for his promotion, so he didn't report the pains. Probably was just indigestion anyway, he thought.

Captain Schrodt threw the throttle levers full forward and the roar of the large jet engines could be heard loudly even in the cockpit. The plane lumbered down the runway, slowly at first, but rapidly picking up speed. After achieving the necessary speed to lift off, Captain Schrodt pulled back on the wheel and the bird was off the ground. Landing gear then stowed, and they were on their way to 35,000 feet altitude. Modern aircraft were capable of automated take-off and landing, but Captain Schrodt, from the old school, always liked to manually accomplish these. Once he achieved cruising altitude, he then would set the auto-pilot and relax.

They had just leveled off at 35,000 feet. Co-pilot Heard, sitting in the right seat, had been watching some air traffic off to his right, but suddenly realized that Don had not yet engaged the auto-pilot. When he turned his head to the left to speak to him he was shocked to see that Don's head was bowed, his chin resting on his chest. Sam quickly reached over to shake Don, but when he did Don slumped over on his left side. It was at that moment that Sam realized Don was totally unconscious. It was also at that exact moment that the tremendous chest pain struck Sam, and he too slumped on his left side, leaning over against the unconscious pilot. The plane was out of control.

After take-off and while they were gaining altitude, Randy and Dom chatted about various flying experiences over the years that they had encountered, and these were numerous. Then, just when the plane leveled off after its climb, they seemed to start going back down. It was just as though the plane went up, reached the top, and then started back down. As much as they had flown, they immediately recognized that something was wrong. This was just not the normal flight pattern. And then they noticed that they appeared to be losing altitude at a greater rate .... the plane seemed to be accelerating down! Looking out the windows they could tell that ground was getting closer, rapidly. And then, all of a sudden the plane leveled in it's flight, and then once again began to rise. It was at that point when Randy noticed how hot his chest felt. He placed his right hand over the Pelle Anchor Cross .... it felt very warm. He then looked over at a very pale Dom, gave him a big smile, and a thumbs-up with his right hand. Randy knew what had happened. Something had caused a problem with the plane that would have resulted in it's destruction, but the Pelle Anchor Cross, exhibiting supernatural power like that of the Seibert Anchor Cross, had somehow prevented the plane crash.

Randy said to Dom, "Well, we wanted to know if the Pelle Anchor Cross was the real thing. I'm here to tell you that it is indeed the real thing. It just somehow saved our lives and all those on this plane. Don't ask me how, but feel my chest." And he placed Don's hand over the Pelle Anchor Cross.

Dom looked at Randy and said, "It feel's hot."

Randy replied, "That, my friend, is what a Savior's Cross feels like just after it transmits some kind of supernatural power to bring about a peaceful resolution to an event threatening the life of the person wearing it. We should say prayers of thanks that one of us was indeed wearing this cross today!"

Stewarts and Stewardesses were running up the aisles of the plane toward the cockpit. The first reaching there began to beat on the cockpit door. Shortly the door opened, and the stewardess looked into the cockpit to see two faces staring back at her with the biggest grins she had ever seen.

She seemed stunned, and almost shouted, "What's going on?"

"Mostly just the automatic pilot right now," said a grinning Captain Schrodt. "Everything's fine. Please just rest at ease. I'm going to make an announcement over the sound system to tell everyone what just happened." And with that Captain Schrodt closed the cockpit door.

"This is your captain speaking," was heard over the sound system. "Let me first assure you that everything is just fine. There is no problem now whatsoever. Sit back in your seats, and let me tell you what I know about the events that just took place. My name is Captain Donald Schrodt. Your Co-Captain is Sam Heard. Everything at take off was normal. I had just gotten the plane to our cruising altitude of 35,000 feet and started to level off when I, for reasons unknown to me, passed out. Co-pilot Heard then looked over at me, and seeing my condition apparently caused him to pass out. A short time later, after the plane had gone down to just under 5,000 feet we both suddenly and unexplainably woke up and again took control of the plane. Another couple of minutes and we would have crashed. We are perfectly fine now, and the plane is back on her way to Atlanta. It is now on auto-pilot, and if for any strange reason the two of us again become incapacitated the plane is programmed to fly to Atlanta and can also land on auto-pilot. We don't anticipate that will be necessary, but for your comfort I wanted you to know. Please relax and enjoy the remaining flight."

Randy looked over at Dom with a smile and said, "Things will indeed be fine now."

Dom nodded, smiled back, and said, "Thanks be to God and to the Pelle Anchor Cross."

•••

Landing in Atlanta was normal. The mob scene in the gate area was not. Apparently the events that occurred on the flight were radioed by the crew to Atlanta and got leaked to the media. As the passengers deplaned they were immediately stormed by television reporters and cameras wanting to know what happened on the flight. Many of the passengers were more than willing to tell their stories, and these soon were plastered on television sets all over America.

Randy and Dom were lucky enough to get around the mob and proceeded to their next gate and flight to Lexington. What a day!

Chapter 12

Muhammad Ahmad, aka Max Robertson, had finally gotten all his things in order, had rented a car for his upcoming trip to Harlan, and had made arrangements for his meager assests to go to his family in the Sudan in the event of his passing, which surely looked likely. He had carefully packed the car with just enough clothes and personal items for his brief stay in Harlan. Because of the explosives packed in his 'special' suit, he did not have the choice of flying to Kentucky. Driving was his only option. And he actually was looking forward to the drive, about 500 miles from Washington, D.C. to Harlan. He anticipated it would take about 8 hours, most of which would be in the state of Virginia. His computer had told him that the trip would take him parallel to the Blue Ridge mountains. He anticipated enjoying the drive.

When he got about 50 miles from Harlan, he stopped for the evening and got a motel. So far on his trip he had just worn jeans and a T shirt, but when he arrived in Harlan he would have to be wearing one of his 'padded' suits in case someone noticed him. So after a relatively good night's sleep and breakfast, he dressed in a padded suit and set out for Harlan.

• • •

Fatso was sitting at the check-out counter reading the **Harlan Daily Enterprise** when the strange car pulled into the parking lot. He glanced up at his monitor showing the security camera's view of the parking lot and noticed the nicely dressed gentleman get out of his car and start walking toward the grocery store entrance.

As the door opened and the bell tinkled Fatso said, "Welcome, welcome. Is there anything I can do to help you mister?"

The stranger said, "Good morning, my name is Max Robertson and I'm here to meet with a Mr. Green."

"I think that can be arranged," replied Fatso. "But first you must pass a test. What did the grape do when the elephant sat on it?"

Mr. Robertson got a blank look on his face, and then replied, "I don't think I understand."

"When the elephant sat on the grape the grape let out a little wine!", Fatso said with a giggle. "I just couldn't resist Mr. Robertson, I love to tell jokes. My name is Fatso Chapel, and I'll see if Mr. Green can see you."

Fatso pressed the intercom button and said, "Hey Trigger, there's a fellow here by the name of Max Robertson to see you."

"Yes, I've been expecting him Fatso, please send him in," Trigger responded.

Fatso pressed the button opening the lock going into the back room that was Trigger's office, and directed Max Robertson to the door.

Trigger was waiting at the door when Max entered. They shook hands, and he said, "Tony Beekins said I should be on the lookout for you, I'm glad you finally made it Mr. Robertson."

"Thank you, please call me Max. I have not personally

met Tony Beekins, but have had many conversations with him via email. Is he presently here in Harlan County?"

Trigger responded, "He is. He's staying in Harlan at the Holiday Inn Express. He told me when you arrived he wanted you to stay with me at my house. I think he was concerned that if you stayed at the motel too many people might see you. It's my understanding that you are wearing a bit of a disguise, and Tony thought that if you stayed with me you could better control your appearance to any strangers that might see you. I must say you do have a bit of an accent .... I don't think people will mistake you as being a Harlan native!"

Max laughed and said, "My original home is indeed quite a distance from here. I think Tony's idea that I stay with you is a good one. I hope it will not inconvenience you too much Trigger."

"No. I'm fine with it. If you're ready I'll take you there and you can get settled in. I'll also call Tony and let him know you're here, and I'm sure he'll want to set up a meeting. You ready to go?" asked Trigger.

"Yes," replied Max, "I'll follow you in my car." Then they walked out of Trigger's office into the grocery store.

Fatso was walking by the door to Trigger's office when it opened and the two walked out. Fatso said, "Hey guys, why do mummies have trouble keeping friends?"

Trigger and Max just kept walking toward the front door.

"Because mummies are so wrapped up in themselves!" said Fatso with a big grin.

"You just have to ignore him," Trigger said to Max.

"I'll be back in about an hour, Fatso," Trigger shouted as they left the store.

•••

After getting Max settled at his home, Trigger returned to his office and called Tony Beekins.

"Hey Tony, Trigger here, your man Max Robertson finally arrived a couple of hours ago. I took him to my house and got him all settled. He wanted to take a nap, so he's there now. Do you want to meet with him?"

Tony replied, "Glad to hear he made it. Yeah, we need to get together. Why don't we plan on meeting there at your store tomorrow morning around 9. That be okay?"

"Sure, got to earn my next $250,000!" said Trigger. "I'll tell you one thing, that Max Robertson is sure a queer looking duck. His face looks all puffy, and he was wearing a suit that looked a bit out of place here in Harlan. Plus, his accent is very strong. You think we can pull it off that he's the new plant manager?"

"Oh we'll do it," replied Tony. "His story is all covered. We'll just have to keep him out of circulation as much as possible until the October 10th ceremony. But I do want him to meet a few people prior to that, so that his appearance at the ceremony is not questioned. We'll talk about that at our meeting tomorrow morning."

With that the two hung up their phones. Trigger rocked back in his chair, put his feet up on his desk, lit a cigar and blew a big ring of smoke and thought, 'That next $250,000 is as good as in the bank'.

Chapter 13

It was mid morning, and Deputy Rosie Cain had Preacher Puss sitting on her desk. Rosie was feeding her *whisker lickins* and stroking her fur. Preacher Puss was terribly spoiled, but greatly appreciated all the attention, and especially the cat treats.

Sheriff Sterling walked into the front office and said, "Rosie, that cat's getting fat. You may have to start rationing the *whisker lickins*."

"Oh Bert, she's just plump. I'd have a hard time limiting her treats," Rosie replied. "And don't forget how she catches criminals for us. She's entitled to her treats."

Bert said, "I should have known better than to suggest anything that might be construed as being negative toward

Preacher Puss. But if she keeps getting all those treats and just lays around this office she'll get big as a tiger. On another note, the mayor just called me and said he wanted to meet. He's coming over here shortly. Just send him on into my office when he gets here."

"Will do," replied Rosie, and she continued to stroke Preacher Puss. The cat had his motor running and was purring loudly.

•••

Mayor Fred Knapp walked into the sheriff's office, "Morning Rosie."

"Morning Mayor, Bert said for you to come on in his office when you got here. Everything well with you today?" asked Rosie.

The mayor walked over to Rosie's desk and gave Preacher Puss several gentle strokes and said, "Yeah, far as I know."

He then walked into the Sheriff's office, "Morning Bert"

"Good morning Fred, you looking good this morning," replied the Sheriff.

"Looks can be deceiving," Fred said. "But I'm in a good mood because I just got through putting on my wall an article out of yesterday's **Enterprise**. It had a picture of a nice elderly lady that lives about five miles up highway 119 toward Cumberland. It was a good story, one worthy of posting on my wall," Fred said with a chuckle.

"I suppose you will now tell me that story," Bert said with a grin.

Fred replied, "Well, if you twist my arm I guess I will. The article was written by a feature reporter for the **Enterprise**. The lady in the picture was 95 years old, and she had just a few weeks ago lost her husband. He was 98 years old. The lady was apparently very well liked and thought of by her neighbors. Her deceased husband was not. He was apparently very cranky and ill tempered, and apparently had no friends. In her interview with the newspaper she shared with the reporter that every time she got into an argument with her husband he would always say, 'When I die, I will dig my way up and out of the grave and come back and haunt you for the rest of your life!'.

And then the husband passed away. Several days after the funeral the widow was talking to one of her neighbors. The neighbor asked the widow if she was not concerned that her husband might indeed do as he threatened....to dig his way up out of the grave and haunt her for the rest of her life. The widow then told the neighbor, 'No, not at all. Let him dig. I had him buried upside down .... and I know he won't ask for directions!'. "

The Sheriff roared with laughter, and said, "I bet that reporter was a woman!"

"Yeah, likely," Fred replied. "But it was a good story. That, however, is not what I came over for. I wanted to chat with you about your progress on security for Senator McDonald's October 10 speech. It's getting closer, and I want to be sure we have everything covered."

"Sure, Mayor," Bert replied. "I think we have things pretty much lined up. The Kentucky State Police have assured me that they will have 10 troopers here. The plan is that these troopers will generally be used in the crowd to assure order. One will be on the platform with the speakers. The other 9 will be stationed throughout the audience. The Harlan City police will take care of the traffic. We plan to rope off the section of Central Street in front of the Court House, and the city police will direct traffic around this closed section. Myself and Deputy Kyle Potter will accompany the speakers to make sure no one confronts them. As far as I can determine right now there will likely be 6 speakers. The governor and his economic development secretary will each speak briefly after I welcome everyone. Then Senator McDonald, and the owner and plant manager of the new company will talk. Of course the Senator will likely take the most time."

"Have you met the owner and plant manager?" asked Bert.

"No, but I've talked with the owner, a Mr. Anthony Beekins. He's staying at the Holiday Inn Express here in Harlan. He called to introduce himself, and said he would like to meet with me, and asked if he and his plant manager could drop by Creech Cafe tomorrow around 3 pm. I told him if they could make it before school got out it would be a lot quieter, so the plan now is that they will come around 11 am."

"Would you mind if I met with you?" Bert asked.

"I was hoping that you would, Bert," replied the Mayor.

"I'm still not 100% on board about this whole thing, although the Senator's office claims to have run checks on both Beekins and his plant manager, a Mr. Max Robertson, and they both check out as being who they claim to be. But I would especially like you there to meet them and then get your take."

"I'll put it on my schedule now, Mayor, 11 am tomorrow at Creech Cafe," said Bert, as he penciled it on his schedule book.

Bert continued, "The thing that concerns me most is their tie to the Maggard Grocery property. I know it is a fact that Trigger Green does have over 4 acres of land there that is currently unoccupied. And I also know that road frontage flat land such as he has is difficult to find. But, as you and everyone else in Harlan County knows, Trigger Green runs lots of illegal operations. We just have not been able to gather enough evidence to close him down. So it concerns me that this Mr. Beekins wants to locate his plant on the Maggard property."

"I see," said the Mayor. "Anything illegal about it, or even out of the ordinary?"

"Not that I've been able to establish," replied Bert. "And

Beekins may be on the up and up, but I'll look forward to meeting him tomorrow to get a few questions answered."

"Good," Fred responded. "I'll see you tomorrow around 11."

Chapter 14

Randy and Dom had arrived in Lexington without incident on their flight from Atlanta. They arrived at Randy's home in the Lexington subdivision called Hartland. Although it was late and they were very tired from their trip, they were too excited to immediately go to bed. Randy fixed them a cup of hot chocolate, and they sat in his living room.

"I've traveled more than my share," commented Dom, "but I've never had a trip as exciting as the one we just completed!"

"It was one for the books," replied Randy. "And although we'll still go through with the testing on the Pelle Anchor Cross to confirm that it is one of the Savior's Crosses, the events on our flight confirmed in my mind the authenticity of the cross."

Dom replied, "For sure. After thinking about things, what is your opinion as to what exactly took place?"

Randy said, "Hard to know for sure until the FAA investigation is concluded, and even then we may well not know. But I think it likely that both the pilot and copilot encountered the unthinkable ..... simultaneous heart attacks. Just from what the captain said, something happened to him first, and then when the co-captain saw him it apparently triggered his heart attack. Then the aircraft and everyone on it were destined for destruction. And we are the only two people that know that the Pelle Anchor Cross then caused the pilot and copilot to regain consciousness and control of the aircraft. Also, I think I know that the details of exactly how that happened will never be known."

"Do we have a responsibility to contact the FAA to give them all the facts as we know them?" asked Dom.

"I think we do," replied Randy. "After we get rested up I'll call them to ask if we could meet with them to give a statement, and also ask if we can remain anonymous."

"That would be good. I also feel we should report what we know, but I certainly would not like to be identified if it could possibly be avoided," said Dom.

"I understand. We'll contact them tomorrow," said Randy.

The two finished their hot chocolates, and then decided to finally retire.

•••

The next morning, Dom accompanied Randy to his office at the University of Kentucky's Center for Appalachian Research. Randy introduced Dom to Joyce, his secretary, and then gave him a tour of his Center.

When Dom saw the Seibert Anchor Cross in it's beautiful display case he said, "Randy, it's a dead ringer for the Pelle Anchor Cross. This just further substantiates my feeling that the two are Savior's Crosses." Dom then walked all around the room reading the accounts known about the Seibert Anchor Cross from it's Harlan County finding and from the further research that Randy had done.

After a while Dom said, "Randy, all this is just so

fascinating. I think one place I would certainly want to visit while I'm here is Harlan. Do you think we might be able to squeeze in a trip there?"

"Funny you should say that," replied Randy. "While you and Joyce were chatting, I checked my messages and found one from my good friend Harlan County Sheriff J. Bert Sterling asking that I give him a call. After you finish looking around here, we'll go back to my office and I'll give the Sheriff a call and see what's up. One way or another I feel certain we'll make a trip to Harlan."

After completing his visit to the Seibert Anchor Cross room, Dom and Randy returned to his office.

Randy hit his intercom and said, "Joyce, would you please try and get Sheriff Sterling on the phone for me."

After a bit Joyce rang Randy and said, "He's on line one."

Randy hit the line one button on his phone and said, "Good morning Sheriff, everything calm in Harlan County this morning?"

"Hey Randy," said the Sheriff, "Good to hear your voice, and glad you're back in town. I understand you were out of the country for a while."

"Yeah, had a little trip to Italy. It proved to be most interesting, and I'll look forward to telling you all about it when we next get together. For the time being, however, if you will permit me I'll put you on my speaker phone. I have with me here in my office Mr. Domenico Pelle. Friends call him Dom, and I know he'll want you to. Dom accompanied me back from Italy. His story is also too long to discuss by phone, but we would like to come to Harlan at some point to visit with you."

"I'm very pleased to meet you via phone Sheriff Sterling," Dom said.

"Likewise," replied Bert. "Please call me Bert."

The Sheriff continued, "You probably received my request for you to call me Randy. The reason concerns an event that we have coming up here in Harlan on October 10th. Senator Rich McDonald, along with the governor, are going to be here to make an announcement about a new plant that will be built here that will employ about 50 persons. When the governor and his staff got word of this they wanted to try and get as much publicity for it as possible, trying to draw a big crowd and lots of media coverage. They then asked me to try and have the Seibert

Anchor Cross here to be on display. They thought that would certainly draw a lot of attention and get a big crowd for the event. What do you think? I told the governor's people I would get back to them after talking with you."

"Interesting," said Randy. "It would be the first time the Seibert Anchor Cross left the Center since it was brought here. But if the governor has requested it, I think we should try and make it happen. My trip to Italy and Dom's being here with me both relate to the Seibert Anchor Cross. I think you should respond to the governor that we'll plan to have the Seibert Anchor Cross there on October 10th, but I think Dom and myself need to come to Harlan to bring you up to date on things. If agreeable with you and Dom, I think I'd like to do that soon."

Dom nodded in agreement, and Sheriff Sterling said, "Absolutely, I know you just got back in town, how about day after tomorrow, Thursday?"

Randy replied, "I think we could make that happen, Bert. We'll plan to see you Thursday around 11 am in your office if that's okay."

"Look forward to it. And look forward to meeting you Dom," replied Bert.

"Same here," Dom responded.

"See you Thursday, Bert. Take care," and Randy ended the phone call.

Randy looked at Dom and said, "Well, our trip to Harlan got scheduled pretty fast! Now I need to contact the FAA and try and get a meeting with them either this afternoon or tomorrow."

Randy then went to his computer and located the phone number for the local FAA office. He then took out his cell phone and gave them a call. After explaining why he was calling, and getting transferred a couple of times, he finally was talking with a manager in the Louisville office. After understanding the circumstances, the manager agreed to come to Lexington to meet with Dom and Randy the next day.

Randy then asked Dom if he would like to go out for lunch and then a little tour of the Lexington area. Dom readily agreed.

After lunch at one of Lexington's favorite restaurants, Randy drove Dom all around the city. They passed the historic Transylvania University as they drove on North Broadway. Thomas Jefferson was governor of Virginia when that state's legislature chartered Transylvania in 1780. When Kentucky then became a state in 1792, Transylvania had already earned the reputation of offering a first-class education. Randy pointed out many of the famed blue grass farms around Lexington, including the world famous Calumet farm. While on Man-O-War Boulevard, Randy pointed out his church, Anchor Baptist Church. Dom responded that it was a beautiful church, and Randy promised to take him to a service there. After their tour, Randy dropped Dom off back at his home. Dom said he needed to do some work using Randy's home computer, and Randy returned to his U.K. Center for the rest of the afternoon.

•••

Randy and Dom arrived at UK the next morning around 8:30 am. The appointment with the FAA folks was scheduled for 10:30 am.

Randy's intercom buzzed at 10:25, and Joyce said, "There are two people from the FAA here to see you Dr. Peters."

"Please show them in," Randy replied, as he and Dom stood to greet the visitors.

The two entered Randy's office. "My name is Val Simmons, and my associate here is John Currens," said a nicely dressed lady as they extended hands to Randy and Dom.

All introduced themselves, shook hands and sat.

"I appreciate your taking the time to meet with us, and for driving all the way from Louisville," said Randy.

"Believe me, Dr. Peters, when we heard your reason for this meeting we were most anxious to meet," said Ms. Simmons. John Currens nodding in agreement.

Randy then explained all the circumstances of his and Dom's presence on the flight. After doing so, he removed the Pelle Anchor Cross from his desk drawer and held it up.

The mouths of Ms. Simmons and Mr. Currens both dropped open simultaneously and their eyes widened.

Mr. Currens said, "That is the most beautiful artifact I have ever seen."

Ms. Simmons, still startled by its beauty, said "It looks very much like the pictures I saw several years ago in the newspapers and on television of what was called the Seibert Anchor Cross."

Randy replied, "Your memory is excellent. This cross, the Pelle Anchor Cross, and the Seibert Anchor Cross, which resides here in the Center, are identical as far as we can determine."

And then Randy further described all the events that occurred on their flight, including the heating of the Pelle Anchor Cross simultaneous with the recovery of the airplane from its pending doom.

Mr. Currens then commented, "Dr. Peters, I feel certain what you have just described took place just as you said. So I think it likely that some unexplainable, mysterious power somehow funneled through that anchor cross brought back to consciousness the cockpit crew of that aircraft. And as a Christian believer, I personally think the event was orchestrated from above, but we can only state your story in our report. There is no way we can confirm the cause and effect between the Pelle Anchor Cross and the Pilots' recovery. I hope you understand."

Randy said, "Yes, I do understand. Dom and I just felt

obligated to report to you what we believe happened. And we have now done that. We would also like to request that our names not be included in any release to the media."

Ms. Simmons then replied, "I think we can honor that request. We will have to release information about the flight to the public very soon. But we will not include your names or reference to the Pelle Anchor Cross. Our report will likely just state that the pilots recovered from a brief 'blackout' just in time to save the plane from crashing. Since there is no way we could confirm a definite link between the Pelle Anchor Cross and the pilots' recovery, your story and explanation will remain confidential in our files. We do thank you very much for putting this information to record."

"I think we all feel much better now," said Randy.

All four stood and said their good-byes, and the FAA couple left Randy's office.

Chapter 15

Trigger and Max arose early, had breakfast, and were waiting for Tony when he arrived at Trigger's home.

"Care for coffee, or something to eat, Tony," asked Trigger.

"Thanks, but the Holiday Inn Express has a pretty good continental breakfast.....so I think I'm good for a while," replied Tony. "You guys ready to roll?"

"I think we are," said Trigger. "Ole Max here sure looks fat in that stuffed suit, but I do understand it's necessary."

Max said, "It's hot as hell, too. But I gotta do what I gotta do!"

"Yeah," Tony replied, "I don't like wearing one either, but we've got to dress the part for the mayor this morning.

Let's hit the road. Max can ride with me, and we'll follow you to Maggard's grocery. We'll do a little more planning there before Max and I head to town to meet the Mayor."

Fatso saw the two cars pull into the grocery store parking lot. All three entered the store at the same time.

Fatso greeted them, "Top of the morning, boys. Do you know why skeletons don't go out on the town?"

The three continued walking through the store toward the door to Trigger's office.

Fatso said, "Because they don't have any body to go out with!" He giggled as he pushed the button to release the lock to Trigger's office.

The three entered Trigger's office and slammed the door shut.

"How do you take that guy?" Tony asked Trigger.

"I'm sort of numb to him," replied Trigger. "He really does a good job with the grocery store front, and other than the corny jokes he's okay."

After all three took seats Trigger asked, "So I understand you two have a meeting shortly with the Mayor in Harlan.... what else is new?"

Tony said, "Everything is shaping up nicely. I got a call from the governor's office this morning saying that something called the Seibert Anchor Cross will be on display at the time of the Senator's speech, and they seemed to think that would help to draw a big crowd. You know anything about the cross?'

"Oh yes, I sure do," said Trigger. "I don't know how it happened, but somehow that cross was responsible for the botched bank robbery here in Harlan about 12 years ago, and for Pretty Boy losing three and a half million dollars. Deputy Kyle Potter actually found the cross in some old ruins, and it got top billing on all the television stations and in all the newspapers for several days following the attempted robbery. So, yeah, it sure is well known to people in Harlan County, and it will indeed draw a big crowd. Does that hamper your plans?"

"No," replied Tony. "Everything goes exactly as planned. The fact that there are more people there won't matter at all."

"Well, I don't mean to rush you, but it's 10:15 and if you're to meet the Mayor at 11 you probably should be on your way," Trigger said.

Tony replied, "Yeah, we don't want to keep the Mayor waiting."

All three stood, and Tony and Max headed out the door of Trigger's office into the grocery store.

Fatso shouted, "What's the same size and shape as an elephant but weighs nothing?"

Tony and Max were almost out the front door.

"An elephant's shadow!" replied Fatso, as he heard the front door slam.

•••

Tony and Max arrived at Creech Cafe about 5 minutes before the scheduled 11 am meeting with Mayor Knapp. They found parking at a metered space and parked, put money in the meter, and walked into Creech Cafe exactly at 11 am.

"New customers, new customers," squawked Polly as she looked at the two from her perch over the door.

"These Americans are strange," whispered Tony to Max under his breath. "Damn parrot in a restaurant."

The two looked around and walked to an empty table

and had a seat. Fred Knapp walked up immediately, stuck out his hand, and said, "My bet is that you are Mr. Beekins and Mr. Robertson .... I'm Mayor Fred Knapp. Welcome to my establishment."

The two shook the Mayor's hand, and Tony said, "I'm Tony Beekins, the owner of the company, and this is my new plant manager, Mr. Max Robertson. Max is originally from South Africa, but has lived in Mexico for the past 5 years working at my plant there. His English is not very good, so I'll do most of the talking."

"I understand," Fred replied. "Well, can I get you coffee or anything else to drink or eat? I'm expecting Sheriff J. Bert Sterling to be joining us, if that's okay with you."

Tony said, "We had breakfast not long ago, but coffee sounds good. May I ask why the Sheriff will be joining us?"

Fred poured coffee and said, "Bert is involved with security control for the Ocotber 10th event, and I wanted him to meet you two. He and his deputy, Kyle Potter, will be escorting all the speakers that day to make sure all goes smoothly. He should be along shortly."

Just then they heard the front door bell jingle and Polly

said, "Howdy Sheriff, Howdy Sheriff". Bert reached up to the perch and gave Polly a stroke, then he walked over to the table where the Mayor and strangers were seated and introduced himself to them.

The Sheriff then said, "Not too often we get gents dressed in suits here in Harlan, and when we do it usually means trouble because they are likely lawyers."

Bert and Fred laughed. Tony and Max looked at each other, and then Tony said with a smile, "I understand your joke Sheriff, but Max here does not understand or speak English every well. Please forgive him."

"No problem at all," Fred replied. "Does Max work at a plant in Mexico similar to the one that you have planned for Harlan?"

"Exactly," Tony said. "He has been in training at the Mexico plant for the past 5 years and understands all the technicalities and manufacturing aspects of producing the computer parts. He will have office staff that will assist him with all the paperwork, hiring of employees, etc. Max's background is in engineering, and he will be responsible for producing a quality product."

"I see," the Sheriff replied. "I had a question about how

you chose the property where the plant will be built. Did you know Trigger Green prior to selecting that property?"

"No," lied Tony. "My company sent a person to Harlan several months ago to seek a suitable location. That person spent almost a week here driving around and checking availability. The Maggard property met all our requirements, and after then contacting the owner, Mr. Green, we reached an agreement on leasing his property. Trigger has been most helpful, and even allowed Max to stay at his home while he's working here. Max and I think the Maggard property will work very nicely for our operation."

Max nodded in agreement and said, "Yes, it should work fine."

Tony continued, "I talked with the governor's staff just this morning and learned that they were successful in getting an article called the Seibert Anchor Cross, apparently well known to most all here in Harlan County, to be displayed at the ceremony on the 10th in order to assure a large crowd. Are you aware of this?"

The Sheriff replied by saying, "I am aware. Dr. Randy Peters called me yesterday from Lexington. He is the person in charge of the Seibert Anchor Cross, and told me of the governor's request."

Mayor Knapp then added, "Yes, I too am aware of it. The governor's staff contacted me also late yesterday to let me know. This will cause a few added problems with security, since the artifact is very, very valuable, but the governor wanted it there, and what the governor wants the governor gets."

Tony then said, "It seems to me that the whole event is being made a bit like a circus with the addition of the cross, but I don't see any harm in having it if it assures a good crowd."

Mayor Knapp continued, "Gentlemen, how long do you anticipate it will take to build the plant and to then hire the 50 or so required people for it?"

"It should be completed in about 9 months from groundbreaking," Tony replied. "We have all the equipment on order, and delivery will be made just as soon as we're under roof. I think it would be safe to say that one year from the October 10th announcement we should be producing product. You agree Max?"

Max nodded his head in agreement, and added, "One year, yes."

Fred then said, "I've checked with the permit people and they tell me all your paperwork is in order to go ahead with groundbreaking as soon as you wish after our announcement. You know where I am, and I'm sure I speak for the Sheriff here when I say we stand ready to assist you in any way to help make your investment in Harlan County a big success."

The four continued to talk about the new plant for another 30 minutes, and then Tony and Max excused themselves and left.

•••

Fred and Bert remained at the table sipping coffee.

Fred said, "So, Bert, what'd you think?"

Bert replied, "I guess it went okay. If they are not for real they certainly put on a good act. The one thing that bothered me a bit was learning that Max was staying with Trigger Green. I'm just real suspicious of anything Trigger is into, and it seems awfully cozy for the new plant manager to be staying at his house."

"Oh, Bert, you're just being too cautious," replied the

Mayor. "I know Trigger is a bad egg, but I'm sure he's getting a bundle for leasing that land. So maybe he's just trying to stay on their good side. I'm sure that it is convenient for Max to be able to be in close contact with Trigger to ask questions concerning the property, etc. I would not think that arrangement was necessarily unusual."

"You're probably right, Mayor," Bert replied. "So I guess on balance everything looks okay. But I'll continue to watch Trigger, and if I see anything unusual regarding this new plant I'll let you know."

"Good enough," Fred responded.

Fred continued, "Now let's talk a little about this new development of Randy's bringing the Seibert Anchor Cross to the ceremony. I must say that came as a bit of a shock to me. I never thought the cross would leave Randy's Center in Lexington. But I should have known that when the governor makes a request, it usually is granted. Are you really okay with all this, Bert?"

"Have to be," Bert replied. "But I do think we can handle it. There are concerns. That cross is absolutely priceless, and the public is well aware of not only it's monetary value, but also of it's reputation for protecting anyone possessing it. There are a lot of crooks and nuts out there, and when this hits the media, which it will real soon, I'm afraid some of those will show up on October 10. But with the help from the State Police I feel we can control everything."

"Really appreciate all your assistance on this," Fred stated. "If you need anything that I can provide just let me know."

Thanks Mayor," Bert said as he stood and patted Fred on the back as he walked out.

•••

Tony and Max arrived back at Maggard's grocery, and fortunately for them Fatso was on the phone when they entered the store, so they were spared his corny joke. He pressed the button to allow them to enter Trigger's office, and they opened the door.

"Hey boys," Trigger said, "good to see you back. I was just wondering about your meeting with the Mayor. Everything go okay?"

Tony replied, "I guess so. He had the Sheriff there to sit in on our meeting. But everything seemed in order, and I didn't detect anything that seemed to alarm either of them."

"Good, good," Trigger replied. "Max, everything okay with you?"

"Yes," replied Max

"Well, you boys have now been introduced to the Mayor of our fine city and to the Sheriff of our fine county, so it seems to me that we just need to play our cards correctly between now and October 10 and all will be accomplished," Trigger replied.

"We just wanted to report to you the results of our meeting," Tony told Trigger as he and Max stood and walked for the door.

They had gotten almost to the front door in the grocery store when Fatso hung up the phone and shouted to them, "You boys know why elephants are grey?"

"So you can tell them apart from canaries!" Fatso answered with a chuckle.

Tony and Max slammed the front door on their way out.

Chapter 16

Thursday morning Randy and Dom rose early in preparation for their trip to Harlan. After breakfast they started their 3 hour drive to Southeastern Kentucky. They had finished their tests of the Pelle Anchor Cross, and the results established beyond a doubt that it was indeed one of the Savior's Crosses that Constantine the Great had created around 325 AD. This morning Randy wore the Pelle Anchor Cross around his neck under his sweater and well concealed by his sport coat.

"Dom, the road we are following this morning overlaps in many places the Wilderness Trail that Daniel Boone and many of the early settlers followed after passing through Cumberland Gap. Every time I make this drive I think about it. The hardships they had to endure are difficult to grasp today as we zip down interstate 75 at 70 miles per hour!"

Dom replied, "Things certainly do change. And not always for the better, although in this case I think I would certainly prefer to be seated in this comfortable automobile going 70 miles per hour rather than in a bumpy covered wagon making 1-3 miles per hour, maybe!"

The two men enjoyed greatly taking in the beautiful countryside as they journeyed South. It also gave them additional time to get to know each other better.

Then Randy said, "Here's our exit, #29 at Corbin. Just right down the road a couple of miles is where Colonel Harland Sanders of Kentucky Fried Chicken fame got his start. His original restaurant is located there. I met folks in Harlan that knew the Colonel, and said they used to visit him at that restaurant. He always stood at the cash register, and always had the image of a Kentucky Colonel, complete with the famous white mustache and goatee. He was quite a character, as well as an excellent chicken chef! One story I recall about the Colonel was that he offered a lot of scholarships after he had made his fortune. One of the requirements for a kid to receive one of his scholarships was that they had to sign a statement that they did not and would not smoke. The Colonel said that if a kid wanted to burn up money under his nose it wouldn't be his."

Dom laughed and replied, "A good one. I think I read somewhere that he was the world's most recognized figure."

"I think that's right," Randy said. "His face is everywhere, including all foreign countries where I've traveled."

"I can recall having many meals of Kentucky Fried Chicken at my home in Italy. Of course I did have a glass or two of fine Pelle wine with the chicken!" said Dom.

"I'm sure that added greatly to the taste," commented Randy.

Randy continued, "Another little tidbit of information about the Colonel is that he and his wife, Claudia, attempted to start another food franchise after the Colonel had sold his interest in KFC. Several restaurants were opened in Kentucky under the name of 'The Colonel's Lady'. These featured lots of excellent southern style vegetables and many different meats, including, of course, fried chicken. For whatever reason, these did not develop as a franchise, and currently all are closed except for one in Shelbyville, Kentucky, not far from Louisville on Interstate 64. This restaurant, renamed as 'Claudia Sanders Dinner House', is located on the Colonel's farm where he and Claudia lived for many years. I stop there frequently when going to Louisville. The food is superb."

"I would love to visit there, maybe I could introduce them to Pelle wine," Dom said with a grin.

"Perhaps we can get there during your stay," said Randy.

The two continued their journey to Harlan on highway 25E South to Pineville, and then turned left onto highway 119 to Harlan.

30 minutes later after they passed the road going to Wallins Randy said, "That grocery store there on the right is called Maggard's Grocery. It was the front business for Pretty Boy Maggard who lost the 3.5 million dollars of illegal drug money during the episode I told you about involving the Seibert Anchor Cross and the botched bank robbery of 12 years ago. Looks like the place has reopened now.....under new management I'm sure!"

•••

Just as Randy and Dom were passing Maggard's Grocery, Tony Beekins was parking in front of the store. He got out of his car and entered the front door. Fatso greeted him, "Good morning Tony, good to see you again. I bet you're not here to purchase any of my fine groceries..... am I right?"

"Just press the button, Fatso, I've got business with Trigger," replied Tony.

"Certainly, Tony, but do you know why elephants have flat feet?" asked Fatso.

"No clue," Tony replied.

"They have flat feet from jumping out of tall trees!" Fatso said with a laugh.

Tony opened the door into Trigger's office and entered.

Trigger, sitting at his desk, said, "Well, well, my favorite contract employer has graced my humble establishment once again. Please have a seat my friend. May I get you some coffee?"

"That would be nice," Tony replied. "I need something

after being subjected to another of Fatso's jokes. Maybe the caffeine will help."

Trigger poured Tony a mug of coffee and again took his seat.

"Where's Max?" Tony Asked

"Sleeping in," Trigger replied. "He does a lot of that. So what's up?"

"I felt we needed to discuss how things are going to go down on October 10th," replied Tony. "I know when I talked with you about Max I told you he would be in a bit of a disguise because he actually worked for Senator's McDonald in Washington on his research staff, and we were afraid the Senator might recognize him unless we altered his appearance. So we came up with the stuffed suits, the medicine to make him have a puffy face, and the wig with streaks of grey hair. And all of that is true. But there was one little detail that I left out. And that was the exact method that would be used to eliminate the Senator."

"Yeah, I assumed Max would have a pistol and some plan to shoot the Senator and then the two of you escape from the ceremony. I didn't ask for any details because that's really none of my business," replied Trigger.

"Of course," Tony replied. "But since the governor got involved and all this stuff about a Dr. Peters' bringing a golden anchor cross to the ceremony, I thought I'd better level with you about how things are going to go down."

"I appreciate that, Tony," Trigger said.

"Well, Trigger, the fact is, Max is actually a suicide bomber!" Tony admitted.

Trigger's mouth fell open and he turned white as a ghost.

"Holy Shit," Trigger finally mumbled. "There's not enough money in the world to get me to go along with that! Why, in addition to the Senator, that would involve taking out the governor, his development secretary, the Mayor, Dr. Randy Peters, likely the sheriff and one or more deputies, and who knows who else. Hey Tony, we're talking a whole new game here. To take out a United States Senator is bad enough, but all these other people as well? No way. Why that'd be on the same order as nine eleven."

"I knew that might be your reaction," replied Tony, "and that's why I came to talk this morning. I would certainly have preferred that all these other people were not involved, but the way things have developed I have no choice. The

$500,000 that you are receiving just for helping make our story legit is a pretty good chunk of change. You will be able to claim complete innocence. You can say that your were hoodwinked just like the Mayor and all the others here in Harlan. They won't be able to prove a thing on you. You'll be totally in the clear."

"Maybe, and maybe not," replied Trigger. "This thing just got cranked up several orders of magnitude. I'll have to think about it, and I may well have some other demands. This has just changed things all around. And let me ask, if Max is a suicide bomber, where are his explosives? He's staying at my house you know!"

"That I'm well aware of," Tony said. "The suit with the explosives is in the trunk of his rental car. It will be safe there until October 10th."

Trigger said, "Why in the world does he not just plug the Senator with a bullet rather than blowing up himself and half of Harlan?"

Tony said, "My friend, that goes to a much deeper level of understanding. You see, Max Robertson is actually Muhammad Ahmad. He's a native of the Sudan, and is a member of a group called the SPLA, it's a terrorist organization, the Sudan Peoples Liberation Army. As such, he is a devout Muslim, and killing infidels in order to please Allah is what he's all about. So the more people that die in his final act furthers the cause of the SPLA. My employer demands that he be allowed to eliminate the Senator in this way. They have their reasons, and I'm being paid grandly to assist, as are you."

"Wow, I've got to rethink this whole thing," said Trigger.

"The clock is ticking," Tony responded. "One week from Saturday is October 10th. I would hate to think of what might be the consequences if you wanted to now back out of our deal. You better think about that, and I'll be back in touch shortly."

Tony departed.

•••

Randy and Dom arrived in Harlan. Randy parked in a space in front of the Court House, and they walked to the Sheriff's Office.

As they walked in, Randy said to Dom, "It's very important that you meet and greet the most important member of the Sheriff's team. She's sitting right up there on that shelf, and her name is Preacher Puss."

Dom reached up, stroked Preacher Puss, and said, "Glad to meet you Preacher Puss!"

The cat responded with a resounding, "Meow!".

"And then the second most important member of the Sheriff's team is Deputy Rosie Cain," Randy said as he extended his hand to Deputy Cain. "And Rosie, I'd like you to meet my good Italian friend Domenico Pelle .... just call him Dom."

Rosie had a big grin on her face as she shook hands with both Randy and Dom and said, "Any friend of Dr. Peters is a friend of mine and of Preacher Puss! The Sheriff and a lot of your friends are already in his office.....they're expecting you!"

Randy and Dom entered into the Sheriff's private office.

Seated in the office were Pastor Raymond Bell, Carolyn Potter, Deputy Kyle Potter, the Mayor, and the Sheriff. The later stood and said, "Gentlemen, welcome to my humble office. I assume that you are Mr. Pelle," as the sheriff extended his hand to Dom.

"Yes, my name is Domenico Pelle, please call me Dom."

"Thank you," Bert replied. "And please allow me to introduce you to Pastor Raymond Bell, Carolyn Potter, and her son and my deputy, Kyle Potter, and the Mayor of Harlan, Fred Knapp."

All shook hands and then had a seat.

Randy spoke, "I must say, I didn't expect to see such a gathering! I feel certain you will all become good friends with this fine Italian gentleman seated here beside me. Dom and I did not even know of the other's existence just a week or so ago, and now circumstances have made us the best of friends. Dom is very special, and I wanted him to both see my beloved Harlan and to meet you, my friends."

With that Randy told the story of how and why he had gone to Prato, had met Father Giovanni Territo and Dom, their establishing the Pelle Anchor Cross as a twin for the Seibert Anchor Cross, and then their amazing plane trip back to the U.S.

Randy then reached under his sweater and pulled out the Pelle Anchor Cross. He held it in his right hand and said, "Folks, I would like you to meet the Pelle Anchor Cross. Not only have Dom and I had first hand experience of the miraculous power of this anchor cross, but we have established through thorough testing that it is indeed one of Constantine's Savior's Crosses, just as is the Seibert Anchor Cross."

All in the room were speechless. All gazed intently at the wonderfully beautiful and mysterious Pelle Anchor Cross.

Kyle spoke up, "I wore the Seibert Anchor Cross for several weeks, and certainly got well acquainted with it. This cross does indeed appear exactly like the Seibert Anchor Cross.....identical."

Bert said, "Although I had the privilege to also see and hold the Seibert Anchor Cross, I must say that to again see one of these is so very special. You can both see and feel it's beauty and importance. Like the Seibert Anchor Cross, the words **pax tecum** across the horizontal arm of the cross reminds us that the gold from which it was cast was blessed by the Prince of Peace. Just to think that now not one but two of these priceless artifacts have found their way to Harlan. Just boggles the mind."

Pastor Raymond Bell then spoke, "I recall so well the day that Kyle and his mother Carolyn came to my office to tell me the story of Kyle's finding the Seibert Anchor Cross, and then showing it to me and asking my advice as to what they should do. Fortunately, I recommended we contact my good friend Dr. Randy Peters at UK, and he was able to trace the cross all the way back to Constantine the Great. I really appreciate being able to be here today to again view a twin to the Seibert Anchor Cross. And yes indeed Sheriff, it does boggle the mind."

Kyle's mom Carolyn Potter then said, "Kyle and I certainly experienced the special, unspeakable power of the Seibert Anchor Cross. It not only protected me from bodily harm from my drunken ex-husband, but it also somehow was responsible for saving our lives in the attempted bank robbery. Now we learn that there is this second cross also with this special power! Wow!"

The Mayor then spoke, "Friends, I was not as closely associated with the events of 12 years ago as the rest of you, with the exception, of course, of Mr. Pelle. But I recall vividly all the interest that was generated from the Seibert Anchor Cross's discovery by Kyle here in Harlan County and then everything that took place until the miracle at the bank robbery. Harlan was thrust into the national, and even international, spotlight. Now once again a similar anchor cross has found it's way to Harlan. As Mayor I have to ask, can we release this information to the press? What great interest there would be to learn of the Seibert Anchor Cross's twin!"

The Sheriff said, "Fred, I think that call would have to be made by Mr. Pelle and Dr. Peters."

"But of course," replied the Mayor. "What would be your thoughts gentlemen?"

Dom spoke up, "Since the arrival of Randy in Prato and hearing the story of the Seibert Anchor Cross, I understood the importance of the Pelle Anchor Cross. Moreover, since my time spent with Randy, and not just the miracle on the plane trip, but seeing his display of the Seibert Anchor Cross and discussing it's incredible history, I have known that my cross was destined to be revealed. I would certainly not seek any personal publicity, and in fact would request that my association with the cross be minimized …. but I feel that the story of the Pelle Anchor Cross should be told publicly. It is an incredible story, as is the story of the Seibert Anchor Cross."

All nodded in agreement, and then Randy spoke, "Dom, I appreciate so much that statement. I also do understand your desire to remain out of the spotlight, so to speak. You are certainly busy enough with your large vineyard and wine operation, and don't need to have tons of additional distractions. The story of the Pelle Anchor Cross would necessarily involve relating that it had been in your family for generations, but beyond that I think the interest would lie totally with the cross itself. With your permission, I would like to suggest that we set up a press conference to announce the Pelle Anchor Cross, and then to display it, rather than the Seibert Anchor Cross, at the October 10th ceremony with Senator McDonald. I'm sure that after the press conference the interest in folks to see it would be even greater than with the Seibert Anchor Cross, so I would feel certain that the Governor and his people would greatly bless the idea. What do you think?"

Dom spoke up, "I like the idea."

The Mayor said, "Seems good to me, and I certainly think the Governor would go along with it."

"Okay," said Randy, "I suggest we set up a press conference for tomorrow morning if Dom is okay with spending the night here."

Dom replied, "Oh that would be special. Maybe I would be able to see some of the sights here in Harlan."

Fred responded, "Gentlemen, the city of Harlan will have you as our honored guests. I will call the Holiday Inn Express and get you rooms, compliments of the city."

Carolyn then said, "And I would like to invite everyone, plus Pastor Bell's wife Betty, to have dinner with my mother, Mawie, and me this evening. We can show Dom downtown Wallins!"

Everyone laughed, and all nodded in agreement. Everyone in the room other than Dom was familiar with Mawie's cooking, and knew what a great treat it would be.

Dom then said, "I accept, but only if you will allow me to bring Pelle wine for everyone. I just happen to have a few spare bottles I stuck in my suitcase for just such an occasion."

Everyone nodded even stronger in agreement!

Carolyn then said, "See all of you at Mawie's at 7 this evening."

Then all except the Sheriff and Deputy Kyle filed out of the Sheriff's office. As each reached the door they gave Preacher Puss a pet and word of farewell. Preacher Puss purred loudly and swished her tail.

Chapter 17

Ever since Tony's visit Trigger had remained in his office trying to decide what he wanted to do now that he knew Max was a suicide bomber. Trigger knew that he was not the best person in the world, but he also knew that setting off a bomb that would indiscriminately kill and maim perhaps hundreds of people, including the Governor, the Mayor, the Sheriff, and the Senator was really far beyond what he had bargained for. To pop the Senator was surely bad enough, and Trigger thought he could very likely remain in the clear from that. But this suicide bomber thing was totally out of bounds. There was just no way he wanted to be a part of a mass killing like that. The problem, of course, was that he had agreed to the deal with Tony, even though when he agreed to it he had no idea of its magnitude. There just had to be a way out for him.

It was almost closing time for the grocery store, and Fatso was getting everything ready to shut down just as Tony walked back into the store and headed for Trigger's office without a word. Fatso was in no mood for a joke, so he just pressed the button allowing Tony to open the door into Trigger's office.

Trigger looked up from his trance and said, "Didn't think I'd see you again so soon."

Tony replied, "Well I was out running errands and was passing by. I thought you'd likely had enough time to decide if you are going to honor our deal."

Trigger said, "I've been thinking about nothing else since we talked this morning. Yeah, I'll go through with it ..... but I don't like it."

Tony grinned, turned to leave, and said, "That's all I wanted to hear. I'll be back in touch."

He walked back through the grocery store and Fatso shouted, "Have a good evening."

Tony slammed the door, got in his car and drove off.

Trigger sat at his desk with his face in his hands,

thinking. He knew that he'd had no choice but to tell Tony that he'd do it. But he also knew that there was no way he was going to allow Max to bomb all those people. The good thing was that he had time to put together a plan to both fool Tony, get his final $250,000 payment, and also prevent the bombing. He didn't know how he would do it, but he had made up his mind to make it happen.

•••

Sheriff J. Bert Sterling and Deputy Kyle Potter parked their car in front of Mawie's home in Wallins and walked to the front door and pressed the doorbell. They could hear people talking inside the home.

Mawie opened the door and greeted them, "Bert and Kyle, how very good to see the two of you. You're the last to arrive, please do come in and join us."

When they entered the living room they saw Fred Knapp, Pastor Raymond Bell, Dr. Randy Peters, and Dom Pelle all sitting, and Carolyn Potter and Pastor Bell's wife Betty wearing aprons and standing in the doorway to the kitchen. After greeting all, Bert and Kyle joined those assembled in the living room, and Mawie returned to the kitchen along with Carolyn and Betty.

After about 15 minutes of conversation Mawie appeared again in the doorway to the kitchen and said, "I think dinner is served. Please make your way to the dining room and have a seat."

After all 9 people were assembled in the dining room Mawie said, "Pastor Bell, would you be so kind as to bless our gathering and the food?"

After Raymond's prayer all were seated around Mawie's very large dining table. It was filled to capacity with bowls of her wonderful country cooking. She had prepared two meats, fried chicken and country ham, a Caesar salad, superbly seasoned vegetables including green beans, boiled potatoes, and corn pudding. There were two large plates that contained corn bread that had just come from iron skillets in the oven, and then for dessert there was Mawie's outstanding apple pie. To drink all were served southern sweet tea with their meal, and then coffee with the dessert.

As they started their meal Mawie commented, "Dom, I fixed the Caesar salad to add a touch of Italian to the meal!"

Dom laughed and said, "Well, Caesar is certainly Italian!. This table looks just superb, thank you so very much for inviting me to such a wonderful meal."

After finishing the meal and much interesting conversation, Randy said, "Folks, what a delightful meal! I think we should give Mawie and her helpers Carolyn and Betty a big round of applause."

They did, and then Randy added, "Although we've just had the best dessert in Harlan County, we've got one more treat for everyone. Dom brought several bottles of one of his Pelle wines for us to try. So if you will permit me, I'll go in the kitchen and open the bottles and serve."

When all were served with glasses of Pelle wine, Dom said, "If I may propose a toast," and he held his glass high, "to all my wonderful new Kentucky friends, thank you so much for your gracious hospitality."

After sipping the wine and chatting for the next 10 minutes Kyle said, "Dom, I can understand why Pelle vineyards and wine are so successful. This wine is quite good. It has a taste and aroma that reminds me of a wine that I tasted earlier this year when visiting with my friend Jake Keller and his wife Jan. They have a home and a small farm just a few miles from here on the Cumberland River. Jake started growing grapes about 30 years ago, and he has a small vineyard that yields enough grapes each year to make wine for his family and friends. Jake's wine is well known around here as being very good. When I tasted this fine Pelle wine I immediately thought of how similar it is to Jake's wine. And I mean that as a very high compliment."

Dom replied, "That is most interesting. Thank you for the kind words about my wine. That there could be a wine made from grapes grown in this area that tastes like my wine is fascinating to me. If we had time while we're here I would very much like to meet and visit with Mr. Keller, and to perhaps sample his wine."

Randy replied, "We have the press conference tomorrow morning at 10 am. It should only take less than an hour. If you like, we could try and set up a visit with the Kellers first thing after lunch, say around 1 pm. And Kyle, could you go with us?"

Kyle looked at Bert, Bert nodded affirmatively, and Kyle then said, "Sure thing. I'll be at the press conference, and we can grab some lunch after its over and then head to the Kellers. I'll call them in the morning to set it up."

"Wonderful," Dom said. "I would like to again thank each of you for the wonderful evening. And Mawie, I especially thank you for the unforgettable meal. And I certainly extend an open invitation to each of you to visit my home in Italy. It would be an honor to have you."

After chatting for a bit longer, each guest extended their thanks to Mawie and departed.

Chapter 18

Friday morning, October 2, was the start of one of those delightful autumn days in Harlan. The trees in the mountains surrounding the town had leaves that had turned to vibrant colors, primarily yellow and orange. The sun reflecting off the leaves gave them a spectacular brilliance. October was truly a beautiful month in the mountains of Eastern Kentucky.

Sheriff Sterling walked into the office shortly after 8 am. He gave Preacher Puss a nice stroke and said, "Rosie, we've got a busy day. I'll go back and start rearranging stuff in the evidence room so that we can hold our press conference in there. I only anticipate a few media folks will show up, so I think the room will accommodate everyone."

"Kyle's already back there setting up," Rosie replied. "He came in early this morning."

Bert walked into his office and continued through the door to the evidence room.

"Morning Officer Potter," Bert said. "Rosie said you got an early start this morning."

"Yeah, I wanted to help get this room all set up, and then I've got to try and contact Jake Keller to see if he can see Dom, Randy, and me at 1. Folks will likely start to arrive for the press conference between 9:30 and 10."

Bert replied, "Well, looks like the room's in pretty good shape for the press conference. Likely won't be many press, and then we need chairs here at the table for Randy, Dom, the Mayor, and the two of us. I think we're in good shape."

"Seems so," said Kyle. "I'll go try and call Jake Keller."

Bert sat in one of the chairs at the press conference table and sipped his coffee. He was concerned about the safety of the Pelle Anchor Cross at the October 10th ceremony. He felt sure that when word of it got out to the public a large crowd would certainly show up, and he did feel good that there would be 10 State Police troopers there, but still, something as valuable as that golden anchor cross could certainly attract some trouble.

"Morning Sheriff," said a familiar voice. Bert looked toward the door and saw Randy and Dom entering.

"Morning gents," Bert replied. "Just sitting here daydreaming. I think we're good to go for the press conference ..... just as soon as we get some press here."

Randy and Dom walked behind the table and took chairs beside Bert. Randy then reached under his sweater, pulled out the Pelle Anchor Cross, and said, "Well I bet when they see this it will start things popping."

"Oh yeah, I'm sure it will," replied the Sheriff.

Just at that moment Kyle walked back into the room, greeted everyone, and said, "Just got off the phone with Jake Keller. He sounded overjoyed that Mr. Pelle wanted to come to look at his vineyard and sample his wine. Said he and his wife Jan would be looking for us at 1 pm."

Dom said, "Wonderful, I'll sure be looking forward to that."

Mayor Fred Knapp then walked in, spoke to everyone, and had a seat at the table.

Four persons then entered the room and Sheriff Sterling stood and walked to meet them. The first person was a lovely, well dressed lady wearing a big smile. Bert gave Barbara Clark a big hug and said, "Barbara, so good to see you again. It's been a while since you were in Harlan."

"It has been, Sheriff," replied Ms. Clark. "And being a native of Harlan I always welcome the chance to come back here. Thanks for inviting me. You remember my camera man Sam Jenkins?"

Bert shook hands with Sam Jenkins and said, "Sure do, welcome Sam."

"Always enjoy trips to Harlan," replied Sam Jenkins.

Barbara Clark was a television anchor from Lexington's CBS affiliate WKYT television, channel 27. Barbara had grown up in Harlan, was a graduate of Harlan High School, and had started with Channel 27 immediately following her college graduation. She was highly respected and known by most people in Central and Eastern Kentucky.

"Hey Bert, good to see you," said A.J. Sampson, reporter for the ***Harlan Daily Enterprise***.

"Good morning A.J., appreciate your being here," replied Bert with a hand shake.

The last person entering was Tim Bates, a reporter for the **Knoxville News-Sentinel**.

Tim extended his hand to Bert and said, "Good to see you Sheriff. Thanks for letting me know about this press conference."

The media folks all got situated, and Bert again took a seat at the table.

"My watch says about 5 after 10," spoke Bert. "I think we likely have everyone whose coming. So let's get rolling."

Bert continued, "Let me introduce you to these people. I think you already know everyone other than the gentleman sitting at the far end of the table. His name is Domenico Pelle. And I'll let him further tell you about himself in a moment. Beside Dom is Dr. Randy Peters from Lexington. You'll recall that Randy is Director of UK's Center for Appalachian Research. And I know you know Harlan's Mayor Fred Knapp. And the fellow standing there in the back of the room is my deputy, Kyle Potter." All those introduced nodded at the media people and gave them a big smile.

Bert said, "This gathering reminds me of the ones we had about 12 years ago when the Seibert Anchor Cross was discovered here in Harlan County. I know each of you were here to cover those historic events. The purpose of today's press conference relates a bit to that Seibert Anchor Cross. I know you are aware that Dr. Randy Peters is its recognized authority, and currently has possession of the Seibert Anchor Cross in his Center at UK. I also know that each of you are aware of the upcoming ceremony that will take place here in Harlan in front of the Court House a week from tomorrow, October 10th. You might have stumbled over some of the construction for that on your way in. At that ceremony our senior U.S. Senator Rich McDonald will announce a significant new manufacturing plant here in Harlan County, and Governor Shear and his Economic Development Secretary, Helen O'Malley will also be present. There will be another significance presence at that ceremony, and I'm going to now ask Dr. Randy Peters if he would make that announcement. Randy."

Bert slid the microphone down the table to Randy.

Randy then said, "Thanks Bert, and I too want to thank each of you media folks for being here. It does remind me of when we were previously together about 12 years ago."

With that Randy reached under his sport coat and

sweater and pulled out the Pelle Anchor Cross. Both print media reporters immediately grabbed the cameras that hung from their necks and started snapping pictures of Randy holding the anchor cross in front of him. Sam Jenkins zoomed in with his television camera to get a good close up of the golden artifact. Barbara Clark then exclaimed, "The Seibert Anchor Cross!".

All at the table smiled, and Randy said, "Actually, it is not. I'll grant you it looks identical, and I can also tell you that it was made from the same gold as was the Seibert Anchor Cross, and it was made by the same person, Constantine the Great, using the same mold as for the Seibert Anchor Cross. But the Seibert Anchor Cross remains in my Center in Lexington. This, ladies and gentlemen, is what we call the Pelle Anchor Cross. If you will recall from the events of 12 years ago, I related to you how my research had determined that 6 of these beautiful gold anchor crosses were made by Constantine, the Emperor of Rome, using gold given to him by Pope Sylvester I around 325 AD. The six crosses were made from gold held by the church that had been blessed by Jesus Christ and then given to Saint Peter, the first Pope, to help start the church. There were many such bars of gold, we don't know exactly how many, but only one was required to produce the anchor crosses. The gold was called St. Peter's gold, and the crosses were called The Savior's Crosses. The Seibert Anchor Cross was the first of the six to be discovered. Over the past 12 years I have been looking for the other five. On a trip to Italy just a couple of weeks ago I discovered the second Savior's Cross in a church in Prato, Italy. The owner of that cross is Mr. Dom Pelle, sitting here beside me, and I'll let him give you a bit of it's history. Dom."

Randy slid the microphone to Dom.

Dom then related the origin of the Pelle Anchor Cross in his family, and discussed it's being placed in the Santa Maria delle Carceri church in Prato, and how Father Giovanni Territo had been its caretaker for the past 20 years.

Dom then slid the mic back to Randy. And Randy told in detail the story of bringing the Pelle Anchor Cross on the trip to the U.S., including their belief that it prevented the crash of the aircraft.

All the reporters were well aware of the strange events that occurred on that Rome to Atlanta Delta Jet. And they were aware that the FAA had simply announced that for whatever reason the two cockpit crew lost and then recovered consciousness before the plane crashed. And they were now aware of a possible explanation, and were keenly aware of how newsworthy this was.

The cameras again began to pop from the print reporters and the television camera got good footage of all at the table.

The next hour was spent in answering questions from the reporters.

Finally Mayor Fred Knapp said, "Folks, it's approaching lunch hour and I think we've answered your questions. I know this is a big story, but I think we've provided you with about all the information we now have on it. The Pelle Anchor Cross will be on display at the October 10th ceremony here in front of the court house. I would invite you back here next Saturday to cover that event. Thank you for being here."

The media folks said quick good-byes and each was talking on their cell phones to their organizations as they left the Sheriff's office. There would be big breaking news from Harlan this evening.

•••

Fred then invited the Sheriff, Kyle, Randy, and Dom over to Creech Cafe for lunch. Upon entering the group were greeted by Polly, "Howdy boys, Howdy boys."

Bert explained Polly to Dom, who then reached up and stroked Polly's feathers. Polly responded with, "That's good, That's good."

All then took a table and ordered lunch. Dom kept looking around at the walls and all the pictures and newspaper articles posted on them. Finally Fred explained that they represented his hobby of memorializing Harlan people and events. Dom saw a picture of a beautiful white rabbit sitting with his eyes closed in a cage.

"Fred, could you tell me the story behind that beautiful, big white rabbit there," and Dom pointed to the photo on the wall.

Bert, Kyle, and Randy all got big grins on their faces as Fred replied, "Yes Sir, I certainly can."

Fred continued, "That picture was taken about 5 years ago. As it turns out this family that lived near Cumberland had this large, white rabbit as a pet. They kept the rabbit in a pen in their back yard. The next door neighbor had a large Labrador Retriever dog. One morning the neighbor saw his dog carrying the rabbit in it's mouth. The rabbit was dead, and it was filthy dirty. The shocked neighbor knew how much the people next door loved that rabbit, and knew they would blame him for his dog's killing it. He figured the dog dug under the rabbit's pen and got him. So he took the rabbit from the dog, got the water hose and some soap and scrubbed the rabbit sparkling clean, then took a blow dryer and fluffed the rabbits fur, and then placed him back in his pen. He was stiff, so he leaned him against the pen wall. He figured the owners would just think he died a natural death. After the owners got home that evening from work, the neighbor noticed that a large crowd of people had gathered around the rabbit cage. He went out and walked up behind one of them and said, 'what's all the commotion?'. The guy he asked then said, 'Well, my friend here had this rabbit, ole Pinky, and Pinky passed away about a week ago and they buried him in the back yard, but when they got home today they found him like that', and pointed to the rabbit!"

Dom laughed so hard that tears rolled down his cheeks.

Fred had a big, proud look on his face, and Randy, Bert, and Kyle roared with laughter.

Dom finally asked, "My, my Fred, do you have a story like that for every one of these pictures?"

"Pretty much," Fred admitted. "And I just love to tell them. Anytime you want to hear more just come back to visit my little establishment here."

"I'll certainly do that," replied Dom.

Lunch was served. After finishing Kyle, Randy, and Dom excused themselves to drive to the Keller home.

•••

Kyle knocked on the door of Jake and Jan Keller's home. Jan opened the door with a giant smile, and invited the trio inside her home.

After introductions all seated themselves in the living room.

Kyle said, "We're missing Jake."

Jan responded, "Oh he'll be right out, he's been behaving like a school kid since your call this morning, Kyle. He's just so excited to have Mr. Pelle visit here."

Just then Jake walked into the room, and with a booming, cheerful voice said, "Indeed I am excited. It's great to have Kyle and Randy Peters visit, but to have such a world famous wine producer and authority as Domenico Pelle in my home is just about more than I can stand."

And Jake firmly shook hands with the three gentlemen.

Dom replied, "First of all, please call me Dom. Secondly, I am impressed that you have even heard of my name and wines, but I guess that's a result of our export business. But believe me, I am the one thankful to be able to visit with you and your lovely wife Jan. Kyle has told us about your history of making fine wine, and I certainly could not pass up the chance to visit with you after hearing Kyle's resounding endorsements of both you and your wine. Thank you for allowing us to come here today."

Jake said, "Technology is certainly not my long suit, but in recent years I have learned how to peck on the computer and to use the internet. Growing grapes and making wine have been my hobby for over 30 years. I got into it by simply deciding one day to try and grow grapes. I read a lot of books about it, and got what information I could, from the county extension people and anywhere else I could find. And, if I do say so myself, I actually was able to produce a pretty nice grape. Then I just naturally extended the vineyard, and over the years it has grown as I needed more grapes to make the wine that I produce for my family and friends. I've never sold my wine. I make it just for the joy of being able to do it and to be able to give it as gifts to my friends. I will have to admit that the list of my friends has grown quite a bit since I started giving the wine! But back to the computer thing, in more recent years I have studied wines using my computer, and as I did the name of Pelle wines became very well known to me. So that's how I came to learn a bit about you and your successful wine business, Mr. Pelle."

"Well, as I once heard someone say, 'technology is wonderful when it works'," Dom replied. "And certainly it has served you well, and I'm thankful that my wines were of interest to you. As I'm sure you learned, my family goes back a long, long way in the business. My great, great grandfather Romano Pelle actually started my vineyards back around 1867. The Lord has continued to bless my family over the generations, and for that I am more than grateful. I wonder if it would be possible to take a little tour of your vineyard?"

"Oh yes indeed," replied Jake. "Jan is insisting that she be able to serve you cheese and Keller wine. So let's go on a tour of the vineyard, and then when we return we'll let you sample the crop."

With that the four gentlemen stood and walked outside. The vineyard stretched from alongside the Cumberland River along a short flatland and then started up the side of a hill. It now covered about an acre.

After walking the vineyard Dom commented, "Very, very impressive. Your devotion to the grape is evident."

Kyle then added, "Just wait till you taste the product, Dom."

Randy said, "In my several visits to Harlan I've had the opportunity to be hosted by Pastor and Betty Bell, Carolyn Potter and Mawie, and Bert and Kyle. It seems they all insisted on serving me a glass of Keller wine, and I can thus certainly add my endorsement to that of Kyle. Just wait till you taste the product!"

"Well, why wait," Jake replied. "Let's head to the house and start sipping!"

After all were back settled down in the living room Jan appeared with a large silver tray of various cheeses. She then returned to the kitchen and brought back another tray with 5 glasses of wine. These she sat on the coffee table, and said, "Gentlemen, I present to you a sample of Jake Keller's wine!"

Dom allowed the others to first sample the cheese and wine, and then after eating a couple of pieces of cheese he smelled as he swirled the wine around in his glass and then sipped.

After a couple of smells and sips his eyes seemed to light up and sparkle, and he said, "It does in fact remind me of home, and of my very own Pelle wine. Astounding! And to think that you've accomplished producing this wonderful wine in only 30 years!"

"I guess the love of my hobby is apparent," Jake replied.

"You bet it is," said Dom. The group then continued the conversation for another 30 minutes while enjoying the cheese and wine.

Finally, Dom said, "I just am flabbergasted. After seeing and tasting what you have accomplished here Jake, I have decided what I would like to do. If you would approve, I would like to get a bottle of your wine and have it shipped overnight to my home. I have, if I do say so myself, a world-class laboratory there for testing wines. I would like them to run an analysis on your wine. If that proves what I think it will, then grape vineyards and wine production could well become Harlan County's new industry."

"Now I'm the one flabbergasted," replied Jake. "I thought I made a pretty good wine, but what you say far exceeded my expectations!"

"We need to wait to hear from the lab," Dom said. "But based on my experience, smell, and taste buds I anticipate very positive results! Randy and I are headed back to Lexington after we leave here. I'll package your wine and get it shipped out overnight express. If all goes well we should hear something back by the first part of next week. I'll be back in contact with you as soon as I know something."

After chatting for another few minutes, Dom, Randy, and Kyle left the Keller home. Jan and Jake were standing on the porch with big grins on their faces and waving as the three departed.

Chapter 19

As Randy and Dom drove back to Lexington they quietly thought about all the events of the past two days. The proposal to show the Pelle Anchor Cross at the October 10 ceremony seemed very well received, and the press conference announcing the latest of the Savior's Crosses to show up in Harlan County seemed to go well. They knew that it would be big news, particularly the inference that the cross was responsible for saving the plane and all its passengers from certain disaster. But perhaps the most important accomplishment of their trip to Harlan was to discover the quality wine made by Jake Keller. As soon as they got back to Lexington Dom would ship a bottle of the wine to his laboratory for analysis. The results from those tests could prove to be a real boom for the economy of Harlan County.

They pulled into the driveway of Randy's home around 5:30 pm. Once inside they got soft drinks and popcorn and got comfortable in the living room to watch the evening news.

At 6:00 pm the first image on the television screen was that of the Pelle Anchor Cross. It's beauty radiated even on television. Barbara Clark's voice then was heard over the image of the cross, "At a press conference held this morning in Harlan, Dr. Randy Peters from UK's Center for Appalachian Research unveiled another of the beautiful and mysterious golden anchor crosses that date back to their being made by Constantine the Great around 325 AD. About 12 years ago the Seibert Anchor Cross was discovered in Harlan County and was the center point of activity that took place there during an attempted bank robbery. The cross you now see looks identical to the Seibert Anchor Cross, but in fact is one called the Pelle Anchor Cross. The name Pelle comes from the cross's current owner, Domenico Pelle."

Dom's face then filled the screen, and Ms. Clark continued, "Mr. Pelle is shown here at the press conference this morning. He is from Prato, Italy and is owner of the famous Pelle wine company. His family, dating back to his great, great grandfather has had possession of this cross."

The camera then showed Dom and Randy sitting at the press conference, and Ms. Clark said, "Dr. Randy Peters, shown here with Mr. Pelle at the press conference, traveled together this week from Italy on the now famous Delta flight from Rome to Atlanta. This was the flight that encountered the strange problem wherein both cockpit crew members passed out and then recovered consciousness just in time to prevent the plane from crashing. Dr. Peters was wearing the Pelle Anchor Cross around his neck at the time, and at the press conference reported that just as the plane recovered from its plunge the Pelle Anchor Cross felt very warm. If you will recall, a similar thing happened to the Seibert Anchor Cross when the attempted bank robbery of 12 years ago failed. At that time the Seibert Anchor Cross being worn by Kyle Potter became quite warm just as he and 3 other persons were about to be locked in an airtight vault that would surely have caused their death. Question:

Could the Pelle Anchor Cross have been responsible for saving the lives of all those aboard that Delta flight?"

The television screen then showed everyone sitting at the press conference as Barbara Clark commented, "That question will likely never be answered, but the coincidence of the two crosses' presence at pending disasters will likely continue as a topic of investigation and discussion. Harlan Mayor Fred Knapp and Harlan County Sheriff J. Bert Sterling then announced that the Pelle Anchor Cross would be on display by Dr. Randy Peters and Domenico Pelle at a ceremony to be held in the Harlan County Court House lawn one week from tomorrow. This ceremony was originally scheduled for the purpose of Senator Rich McDonald's announcing a new plant in Harlan County that would create more than 50 new jobs. Governor Shear and Economic Development Secretary Helen O'Malley will also speak there. I'm sure that with the added presence of the Pelle Anchor Cross there will be a huge gathering in Harlan next Saturday. Channel 27 will be there to bring you all the coverage. Stay tuned."

And then the news moved to other events.

Less than a minute later Randy's phone rang, and the

caller ID showed the source of the call to be the Louisville Courier Journal. Randy let his answering machine pick up, and said, "I think I'll not take any calls this evening, Dom. Why don't we just turn the television off and just relax and talk a while before bed."

Dom nodded agreement and said, "Suits me fine, we can deal with all the phone calls later. It's been a long and eventful day, and I am tired. I'm going to package the bottle of Keller wine for overnight shipment, and we can get it on its way tomorrow morning, and I'm going to call the director of my laboratory to alert him that it's on the way and that we need the analysis done pronto. Then I'm hitting the sack!"

•••

The next morning Randy and Dom awoke about 6 am and after getting themselves ready for the day and drinking several cups of coffee headed to Randy's office. On the way they stopped at a FedEx office to overnight Dom's package to his laboratory.

Since it was Saturday, most all employees were not

working. Joyce, Randy's secretary, was at home, and the office was quiet. Randy returned a number of phone call messages and got caught up a bit on office work, and Dom accomplished several tasks related to his wine business by addressing them using phone, fax, and texting. They worked continuously until almost 5 pm. Then Randy said, "Dom, why don't we call it a day with all the work, and then go enjoy a good dinner."

Dom replied, "Best offer I've had today." They locked up the office and went to dinner.

•••

Sunday morning the two were up early to get ready to go to church. Randy wanted Dom to attend a worship service at his church, Anchor Baptist. The members there were so friendly, and Randy had become good friends with both the senior pastor, Dr. Gus Carl, and the Associate Pastor, Mr. R.T. Kris. The two were well received by members of the congregation at the service and then were able to chat briefly with the two ministers as they left.

After they got in their car and started to drive Randy

then said, "Thanks for going with me to church, Dom. It always really recharges my batteries!"

"My pleasure, Randy," replied Dom. "I too got a blessing from the service. We often times tend to forget the source of all we have. Thanks be to the Lord Jesus Christ!"

"Amen to that," said Randy. "And having attended Anchor Baptist Church reminds me of a couple of Baptist Church related stories. If you'll permit me I'll tell you these stories as we drive to Shelbyville for lunch at Claudia Sanders' restaurant."

"Can't wait," replied Dom.

Randy began, "Well the first has to do with this lady that lived in a large city. She had relatives that lived in the country that she had not visited, and she finally decided to attempt a visit with them. The thing that really bothered this lady concerned the bathroom facilities..... she was very much afraid that the relatives might not have indoor plumbing, and the thought of an outhouse frightened her. And she didn't really know how to go about inquiring about this. Finally, after thinking about it for a while she decided to write them a letter announcing that she would like to visit them and she thought she'd just ask if they had a bathroom with a commode. But she didn't know how to spell commode, so she just abbreviated bathroom with commode as 'BC'. She asked them if they had a BC. When the relatives got the letter they were delighted that she wanted to visit, but when they got to the part that asked if they had a BC they became puzzled. They didn't know what she meant by BC. After a bit, they figured out that she likely meant Baptist Church. So they responded by writing a letter saying how glad they were that she was going to visit them, and yes indeed they did have a BC. They said the BC seated about 200 people, was located about a mile from their house, which could be a problem if she had to go very often, but if she was like them and just went once a week it wasn't too bad."

Dom laughed loudly and said, "I bet that lady never visited her relatives!"

Randy replied, "And then there was this little girl Amanda that was in the 4th grade. Her teacher said they were going to have a 'show and tell' the next day, and each student was to bring something that represented their religion. The next day when time rolled around for the show and tell the teacher first called on Saul. Saul said 'I'm

Jewish, and I brought a Star of David'. Teacher thanked Saul, and then called on Mary. Mary said, 'I'm Catholic and I brought a rosary'. Teacher thanked Mary and then called on Amanda. Amanda said, 'I'm Baptist and I brought a casarole."

To which Dom chuckled and replied, "Well, that sounds about right. Those Baptist do enjoy their casaroles!"

"And now we're getting ready to really enjoy some super fine food at Claudia Sanders. I know you recall my talking about it earlier, so I thought today would be a good time to just relax and have a big country meal and then maybe watch a DVD movie at home later. That sound okay with you?" asked Randy.

"Sounds like a plan to me," replied Dom. "we have a busy week coming up .... so a good restful day today is definitely in order."

Chapter 20

It was Monday morning. Mayor Knapp and Sheriff Sterling were walking around the front lawn of the Harlan County Court House assessing the newly constructed stage for Saturday's ceremony.

"I'll be happy when this whole thing's over," Bert said. "I'm still very concerned with the security issue, and on top of that this stage blocks the main entrance to the court house, making people have to walk around it to get in. But I know it's necessary, so we'll just have to put up with it."

"Yeah, I know your feelings," replied Fred. "I'll be glad to have it over as well. But to have new jobs announced for our depressed county and to have all the dignitaries here in Harlan will certainly be worth the trouble. And now with all the media craze over the Pelle Anchor Cross, and with its presence at the ceremony, I'm certainly not worried about drawing a big crowd. As a matter of fact, I'm now getting concerned that the space available here for people to view the ceremony might not be adequate. What'd you think, Bert?"

Bert replied, "Some of them might not have the best view, but I feel certain that we can handle them. They'll just spill over into the streets. It'll work out."

And then after the two had surveyed everything in front of the court house, they went back to Creech Cafe and continued their conversation over coffee and doughnuts.

Fred said, "Since that press conference last Friday I've been getting phone call after phone call from the media wanting the details for Saturday's ceremony. I've told each of them that it would begin at 11 am, and that the order of speakers would be first a welcome to everyone from myself, then I would introduce everyone on stage, and then the Governor and Secretary would make comments followed by Senator McDonald. He will then ask Anthony Beekins and Max Robertson to speak. I understand the name of the new plant will be AB Enterprises. I guess the AB is for

Anthony Beekins. Following them will be Dr. Randy Peters and Domenico Pelle with remarks about, and the showing of, the Pelle Anchor Cross. You see anything wrong with that order of speakers?"

"No, I think that will be fine," Bert replied. "It will be good to get the business about the new plant out of the way before starting with the Pelle Anchor Cross. When that happens the excitement will crank up a notch, and that's the point where I'm most concerned about some problem developing. At least it will be at the end of the ceremony, and that should minimize its exposure."

Polly flew over to the table where Bert and Fred were sitting and said, "Polly hungry. Polly hungry."

Fred replied, "Too bad. Too bad."

Polly replied, "Polly mad. Polly mad."

"That reminds me of a story," Fred said.

Bert got a grin on his face, and said, "Shoot."

Fred said, "Well, this robber had broken into a home one night when the owners had gone on a trip. The robber had a flash light and was wondering throughout the house when all of a sudden his light shines on this parrot in a cage, and the parrot says, 'Jesus is watching you, Jesus is watching you'. The robber then says to the parrot, 'What's your name, bird?'. The parrot says 'Clarence'. The robber than says, 'What kind of a person would name a parrot Clarence?'. The parrot then says, 'The same guy that named his pit bull Jesus.'"

Bert laughed as Fred giggled. Polly flew back to her perch above the front door.

•••

Dom had accompanied Randy to his office Monday morning. Most of the day had been consumed with phone calls from the media about the Pelle Anchor Cross. Randy would answer for a while, and then let Dom field questions for a while. Around 4 in the afternoon Dom's cell phone rang. It was his laboratory manager in Prato. Dom listened for a moment, and then a big wide grin formed on his face.

"That was the news I'd been expecting, and hoping, to hear," Dom said to Randy.

Randy replied, "From the looks of the grin on your face it was good."

"Sure was," Dom said. "My lab confirmed that the wine was equal in quality to my Pelle wine. This means that Harlan County could very likely develop winemaking as a new industry. Of course it takes several years to produce the grapes that are required, but at least the potential payoff is out there. I personally plan to get some of my people over here to go to Harlan and try and find suitable land to purchase for starting my Pelle, USA operation. Currently all my vineyards and winemaking are at Prato, and I have been thinking for years about trying to begin another vineyard somewhere, but just couldn't find a suitable location. I think I've now found it."

"I'm sure all the folks in Harlan will be super pleased to learn the news," commented Randy. "And also the Governor and his economic development people. Do you think you will announce your intentions at the ceremony Saturday?"

Dom replied, "It would seem logical. Everyone will be there, and they're expecting news about new jobs, so why not let them know what we've uncovered."

"Makes sense to me," replied Randy. "Saturday is certainly shaping up to be a big day."

•••

Trigger and Fatso were huddled in Trigger's office. They kept an eye on the grocery store using the closed circuit camera surveillance. No one was in the grocery store.

Trigger said, "Fatso, I'm really concerned with this deal we've got going with Tony and Max. Things have developed that were just not what I'd bargained for. But at the same time, I think there is an opportunity to make lemonade out of lemons, if you get what I mean."

Fatso replied, "Those two have always bothered me. They seem to be in a league of their own .... not like most of the people we usually deal with. Course I don't know exactly what you have going with them, but if I can help anyway just let me know."

"Thanks Fatso, I am going to need your help. I have a plan that I think will get us out of our dealings with them, and smelling like a rose. The big ceremony this Saturday at the Harlan County Court House will mark the end of our relationship with those two. If things went down as Tony has them planned, then lots and lots of people would be killed. I don't want that. But I do want the remaining

$250,000 payment that Tony owes me. My plan would both get those two off our backs, save the lives of all those people, and would still get us the money."

"Just let me know what you want me to do," Fatso replied.

"That I will," said Trigger.

The two looked up at the closed circuit camera and saw Ms. Johnson walk into the grocery store.

"Better go help Ms. Johnson," Fatso said as he walked into the grocery store.

"Hi Fatso," Ms. Johnson said. "Just needed to pick up a few things."

"You go right ahead, Ms. Johnson. Thanks for coming in," replied Fatso.

After finishing her shopping Ms. Johnson proceeded to check out and placed her groceries on the counter. As he scanned her groceries Fatso said, "Ms. Johnson did you hear about the doctor that treated the guy for yellow jaundice and it turned out he was oriental?" Ms. Johnson got a blank look on her face, paid Fatso, took her groceries and left.

Chapter 21

Sheriff Sterling just hung up the phone talking to the State Police. Everything was in place for Saturday's big event. Today was Wednesday. He had a meeting scheduled for tomorrow with both the Harlan City Police and the Kentucky State Police as a final check to make sure everyone knew their responsibilities.

Bert stood and walked into the front office. He walked over to Preacher Puss and gave her several gentle strokes.

Rosie said, "That cat sure does enjoy life here in the Sheriff's office. She thinks she runs the place."

"Well, it is peaceful," replied Bert. "I'm heading over to see Fred. Where's Kyle?"

Rosie replied, "He got a call to go check a house robbery. Tell Fred 'hi' for me."

"Will do," answered Bert and he then left the Sheriff's office and walked across the street to Creech Cafe.

"Sheriff's here, Sheriff's here," screamed Polly as Bert walked through the door.

Bert reached up and gave the parrot a pet, and then saw Fred with a group of people in the back of the cafe. It looked like Fred was getting ready to start on a story. There were three ladies and one man sitting at a table beside Fred. The four people did not look familiar to Bert. He had a seat at a counter stool close to the group.

Fred said, "Hey folks, the Sheriff of Harlan County just moseyed into my establishment. Bert, these four folks are visiting here in Harlan and heard about my monthly 'About Town' tour and wanted to hear a little about our fine city. They just finished coffee and doughnuts and we were getting ready for the tour when one asked about one of my wall hangings. Folks, I would like for you to meet Sheriff J. Bert Sterling."

"Very pleased to see you here, and glad you're interested in our town. You came to the right place to get informed.

Mayor Knapp knows the city past, present, and future. And in addition to giving an excellent walking tour of our town, he has a lot of its history right here decorating the walls of his cafe," replied the Sheriff.

Fred responded, "Thank you Bert. Do we have some business we need to discuss before I proceed with my story and tour?"

"No, no. You go right ahead. We can talk later, no rush," Bert replied. "As a matter of fact, if you don't object I think I'll listen to your story and then walk along with you for the tour. I need some exercise!"

"Great," replied Fred. He then looked at one of the ladies seated at the table and said, "Now I believe you were asking about the picture up there that is of the young fellow with the big smile holding a ticket."

"Yes," she replied. "He looks so excited."

Fred started, "Well, he was very excited when that picture was taken. You see, his name is Oscar, and ole Oscar came from a very poor family that lived about five miles from here at Cawood. Oscar had read books and studied brochures for years about taking a cruise. Problem was, Oscar was so poor he couldn't even hardly think about it. But the more he read books and studied brochures the more determined he became to somehow take a cruise. So one day he was reading the **Harlan Daily Enterprise** and saw this little ad that said, *Cruise to the Virgin Islands for two weeks for $50*, and there was a phone number to call. Now Oscar had been saving his money for almost 2 years and had saved $60. He got real excited, and called the number. A nice lady answered and told him that all he had to do was get to Miami and go to dock 5A at 6 am on a certain day. He said he'd do it, and mailed her $50. He then got the ticket that he's holding, and that's when his mother snapped the picture."

"So did he go on the cruise?" the lady asked.

Fred continued, "Oh yes he did. He hitchhiked from Harlan to Miami, and on the morning he was supposed to report to the dock he was standing there when two large men grabbed him on either side and carried him aboard the boat. He was taken down below and chained to an oar. There were 200 other men down there, each chained to an oar. They were then told to start rowing. They rowed for one week, just stopping long enough for soup and water. Once they arrived in the Virgin Islands they almost immediately started back. Again they rowed continuously for a week except for brief stops for soup and water. They were then approaching Miami when Oscar looked over at the guy across from him and said, 'Say, this is my first cruise. Are we suppose to tip the soup steward?'. The guy replied, 'I'm not really sure, this is just my second cruise, but I tipped him last year.'"

All four people at the table and the Sheriff laughed so hard that tears rolled down their cheeks.

Bert then said, "I bet Oscar just took one cruise."

"I think you're likely correct," replied the Mayor. "Okay folks, time to stretch those legs. Let's head out for the town tour."

Mayor Fred Knapp had started doing walking tours of Harlan soon after being elected Mayor. He called them *About Town with the Mayor*. The tours were always on the first Wednesday of the month. The **Enterprise** always ran an article about the tour a few days before each one. Some months no one would show up for the tour, and some months there were as many as a dozen. Today there were four, plus the Sheriff. They all walked out onto Central Street and turned right.

Mayor Knapp began talking to the group, "Folks, we are now walking West on Central Street. Directly across the street on your left is the Harlan County Court House and Harlan County Sheriff's office. I think our Court House is a very impressive structure. The Doughboy there in the front of the Court House was placed there in 1930 by Harlan Post No. 54 of the American Legion. The Doughboy is dedicated to the memory of the 30 valiant sons from Harlan County that lost their lives in World War I, 1917-1918."

He then walked the group to the corner of Central and First Street and pointed to a coal monument erected on the Court House lawn at its Northwest corner, fronting First and Central Streets. He said, "That coal monument was built in 1941 by the Harlan Mining Institute and the City of Harlan to commemorate the first shipment of coal by rail from Harlan County, which occurred in August, 1911. Any kids that grew up in Harlan after 1941 will have a memory of coming downtown and sitting on that coal monument. Across First Street from the Coal Monument and a couple of doors South there used to be Moody's Pool Hall. Lots of our male youth from the mid to toward the end of the last century spent a lot of time in that Pool Hall. Beside the Pool Hall was the very popular Charlie Buckner's barber shop."

The group then crossed First Street, and were then standing on the Northwest corner of the intersection of First and Central Streets. Fred continued, "On this corner was a very popular drug store called Green-Miller. It was one of four in downtown Harlan. Creech Drug stood about where Creech Cafe is located today. Howard and Lee Drug Stores were located further down at the next intersection."

Fred then pointed North on First Street and said, "The Harlan Post Office is located up there on the left. Directly across the street from it is a building that was once the Greyhound Bus building."

They continued walking West on Central Street. When about half way down the block Fred said, "Here on my right there was once a men's clothing store operated by a gentleman named D.Y. Turner. Mr. Turner had quite a reputation in Harlan. I guess you would call him a bit of a non-conformist. He had clothes in his store that went back to the early 1900s, and he lived in the back of his store. Across the street there was once a large Belk's department store. For many years the store manager, Mr. 'Wild' Bill Wilson, was a most popular figure in Harlan."

The group continued West on Central until they reached Main Street.

Fred said, "Across the street was Howard Drug Store. And across Main Street from Howard Drug was Lee Drug Store. Here on our right was located a men's clothing store called 'Forester and Spillman', operated by Mr. Bill Forester. Mr. Forester wrote 4 books helping to document the history of Harlan."

As they crossed Main Street Fred said, "The building directly in front of us was for many years the Harlan National Bank." They continued West on Central to Cumberland Avenue.

Fred said, "Here at the corner of Central and Cumberland Avenue was the Coca-Cola Bottling Company for many years. And if you look on down Central Street to the next intersection, and that would be Elm Street, where the VTC bus company was located at one time. Further down, now about where the Gene Goss by pass road is located, was the old Harlan swimming pool. Kids spent many happy hours in that pool during by-gone summers."

The group then crossed Central Street headed South on Cumberland Avenue. About half way down the block Fred commented, "This building here on our left was once the main hotel in Harlan, the Lewallen Hotel. It was owned and operated by a Mr. Ben Lewallen. The four story hotel had a nice coffee shop and 132 rooms."

Continuing South on Cumberland Avenue the group arrived at Clover Street.

"Here at the corner of Cumberland Avenue and Clover Street was Black Motor Company, one of Harlan's larger auto shops," Fred said. "And if you look west there on Clover Street there was once an auto supply store that was operated by Wannamaker Turner. He was the son of D.Y. Turner, the fellow who operated the clothing store on Central Street."

Continuing East on Clover Street the group then arrived back at Main Street. Fred said, "From the 1940s to the end of the century the A&P grocery store was there on the Northeast corner of the intersection. Across the street on the Southeast corner was Bower's Department Store. Across Main Street from Bower's was a little food diner that was adjacent to a cab company called '900 cab'. Mr.

Estil Giles owned the cab company and was the City's Fire Chief for many, many years. Mr. Giles also owned three drive in restaurants here in Harlan. Close to the Northwest corner of this intersection was a restaurant called the Royal Cafe, operated by a Mr. Wilson Adams. And further down North on Main Street, at about the middle of the block, was Powers and Hortons men's clothing store, and across the street from it was the Quality Shop."

As the group proceeded East on Clover Street the Mayor pointed to his right and said, "There where Bower's Department Store once stood is our new Harlan Center. We are very proud of the Center. As you can see, it has lots of parking space and the Center itself is now home to many events that take place in Harlan. The Center has 7,000 square feet of convention floor which can be broken into eight separate rooms for smaller events. The parking lot across from the Center on South Main Street is the location where the New Harlan Theater once stood. The New Harlan and the Margie Grand were the two theaters in downtown Harlan. The Margie Grand was at the corner of Central and Second Streets."

The group soon came to First Street, and there turned North.

Fred said, "There on our right is City Hall. The building was constructed just a few years back when a fire destroyed the old building."

Continuing North on First Street the group soon came back to the Court House on the right and then the intersection with Central Street.

"One last thing I'd like to point out," Fred said, "is that there used to be a restaurant there on our left that was called the Court Cafe. It was operated for years by Wilson Adams, who previously operated the Royal Cafe on Main Street. The food there was great, and Mr. Adams was loved by most in Harlan."

With that the group then walked East on Central Street back to the Creech Cafe. Standing outside his restaurant Fred said, "Folks, it has been a great pleasure to tour you around a bit of Harlan. There's lots more here to see. Please take the time to explore around our little town. Thank you so much for your time and interest!"

The four persons each shook hands with the Mayor and thanked him for the grand tour.

Bert then said, "Fred, you sure give a good tour. Every time I go on it I learn something new about our town. I really appreciate you!"

Fred replied, "Oh Bert, I just enjoy doing it. Harlan is so special to me. Lets go in and get a cup of coffee and talk about whatever it was you came over here to talk about."

Fred and Bert walked into Creech Cafe. Polly was busy mooching food from a customer, so she ignored the two. They walked to a table in the back of the cafe. Fred stopped on the way to grab a carafe of coffee, and after they were seated he poured two cups.

"Before we get started with business Fred, I wanted to make one comment about the tour. You didn't mention the five and dime store Newberry's that used to be located on Main Street between Howard Drug and the Quality Shop. The thing I remember best about that store was each year on the first day of school all the kids would flock to Newberry's to get their school supplies. Especially the younger kids would all have to get pencils, paper, erasers, glue, rulers, colors, etc. The store was always just packed. It was an exciting time."

"Oh boy, I remember that too," Fred replied. "I'll try to

remember to mention Newberry's in my future tours. But that's not the only store I missed. Harlan had lots and lots of stores that were interesting ..... but there's just no way I could include them all."

"Understood," replied Bert. "So now lets talk a little business."

"Shoot," the Mayor replied.

Bert continued, "Got a call earlier today from Randy Peters. I know I told you about Kyle telling me how much Dom liked Jake Keller's wine. Well, Dom overnighted a bottle of it to his laboratory in Prato for analysis, and Randy called me to give us a heads up that the wine checked out to be comparable to his own Pelle wine. Dom has now directed a couple of his people to come to Harlan to begin a search for land suitable for a vineyard. His intention is to start an operation in Harlan County that will expand his Italian business. He further thinks that growing grapes and making wine could be a great boost to Harlan County's economy. He plans to announce this at the gathering on Saturday, unless you see a reason not to."

"I see every reason for him to make the announcement," replied the Mayor. "How often do we have the ear of the

Governor and his Economic Development Secretary as well as that of a United States Senator? Plus there will be all kinds of media there that will spread the word. This could truly be the start of something big, as they say!"

Bert responded, "I'm glad you agree. I told Randy I'd share the news with you and then get back to them. Their plans are to come to Harlan tomorrow. Dom wants to meet with his people regarding the land search, and Randy wants to get all set for his talk introducing the Pelle Anchor Cross. I think he intends to let Dom talk about the wine thing. Maybe we could all get together tomorrow evening for a meal. Raymond Bell needs to be brought up to speed on all these developments. Maybe I could twist his arm for an invitation to dinner tomorrow. Betty is a mighty good cook you know."

"Pastor Bell's place would be perfect for a get together as well as an excellent meal," Fred replied. "Why don't you give Raymond a call and see if he and Betty are agreeable."

"I'll do it first thing when I get back to my office," replied Bert.

The mayor then said, "One last thing before you go Bert, I heard a good story I wanted to share with you."

Bert grinned and said, "I'm all ears!"

Fred replied, "Well, it seems that when the Lord made Adam, and before He made Eve, Adam came to the Lord one day and said, 'Lord, I'm lonely'. The Lord then told Adam that He would solve that problem. He was going to make for Adam the most beautiful, compassionate, intelligent, articulate, caring creature that He had ever made. It would be the absolute pinnacle of His creation. Adam thought about this for a minute, and then asked the Lord 'What's this going to cost me?' The Lord said, 'Well, I think one arm, one leg, one eye, and your left ear should about cover it'. Adam replied, 'What can I get for a rib?'"

After laughing for a minute Bert said, "I guess I now know the real story behind the creation of woman."

"Yeah," replied Fred, "but just don't tell that version to Pastor Bell .... he might not appreciate it!"

Chapter 22

It was now Thursday, October 8th. The big ceremony at the Harlan Court House was now only two days off. Final plans were underway by all concerned.

•••

Tony Beekins and Max Robertson walked into Maggard's grocery. Fatso was sitting at the checkout counter and yelled to the two, "Morning boys. You know why mummies have trouble keeping friends?"

Tony and Max continued their walk toward the door into Trigger Green's office.

"Mummies have trouble keeping friends because

they're so wrapped up in themselves!" continued Fatso with a chuckle. He then pushed the button to open the door into Trigger's office.

"Well, well, looks like the bomb squad has graced my humble office," Trigger said as he sat at his desk. "Have a seat gentlemen."

"You should tone down the jokes Trigger. Having to listen to Fatso every time I come here is bad enough," replied Tony as he and Max pulled up a chair in front of Trigger's desk.

"Oh, a little levity in life is a good thing Tony," Trigger said. "Now what can I do for you two this fine morning?"

"The big show's only two days off, and I thought we'd best go over exactly how everything will come off," said Tony.

"Sounds reasonable," replied Trigger. "Ole Max here needs to know just exactly when and how he's going to meet ole Allah, and cause a big bang!"

Max sat without expression and did not speak. Tony started to get red faced, but then continued, "This is the way things will play out. The Mayor says the ceremony will get underway at 11 am. Max and I will get to the Court House at exactly 11 am. The Mayor told me that we needed to be there about 10:30 in order to meet everyone and get all set for the ceremony, but I know they won't start without us. I don't want to take any chances on something going wrong. Meeting these people and doing the chit-chat could well lead to problems, so we'll come up with some excuse for being late and show up at 11 am. That way we should only have to shake hands with the others in the ceremony, and then we'll all proceed up on the stage and be seated. The Mayor will first say a few words and briefly introduce everyone on stage. Then he will call on the Governor and Economic Development Secretary for comments. Next will come the Senator who will talk about our new plant and the 50 jobs it will bring to Harlan, and then he will introduce me. I will say a few words, and then I'll introduce Max. I'll say that Max speaks little English, and he will simply stand, grin, wave at the crowd, and then again take his seat. At that point I will then say that I will excuse myself from the stage in order to retrieve two suitcases of computer parts that I'll bring back to show the audience. I'll say these parts are similar to those that will be manufactured at the new Harlan plant. I will then depart the stage to head for my car and start back here to Maggard's grocery. The Mayor says that the next person to be introduced for speaking will be a Dr. Randy Peters to talk about something called the Pelle Anchor Cross, and then the final speaker will be an Italian to talk about wine. I don't understand the reason for these two last speakers, but when the Italian finishes his remarks Max will do his thing. At that point I should be on my way back here to give you your final $250,000. After I do that I'll get back in my car and make my final exit. But here's what you need to understand Trigger, the explosion that Max will detonate will be large enough that I will be able to both see and hear it. Once I get outside Harlan I'll pull off the road and wait for the explosion. If for any reason it doesn't happen, then I'll just keep driving past Maggard's grocery and you'll never see me or the $250,000 again. Do you understand?"

Trigger responded, "I hear what you say, but I don't understand what my final $250,000 payment has to do with Max being able to blow up himself and half of Harlan. I've cooperated with you just as we agreed."

Tony said, "You have cooperated so far. But my mission is not complete until the explosion occurs. So if that does not happen, you miss your final pay. That's my insurance policy that you won't try any monkey business. Understood?"

"I guess that makes sense," replied Trigger. He then looked at Max and said, "I hate to say this Max, but I'll sure be glad to see you gone!"

Max sat without expression for a moment, and then said, "Allah's will be done."

•••

At approximately 5 pm Randy and Dom walked into Creech Cafe.

"Howdy boys, Howdy boys," squawked Polly.

The two reached up and stroked Polly, and then walked to a table and sat down. Fred was talking with two customers, and when he saw Randy and Dom he excused himself and walked to their table.

"Good afternoon my friends," Fred boomed. "I trust you had a good trip from Lexington down to Heavenly Harlan!"

Randy said, "It's always a nice trip, and getting into the beautiful mountains of Eastern Kentucky adds a lot to the enjoyment. But we could use a cup of that good Creech's coffee."

"Coming right up," Fred replied. "But I thought maybe Dom brought some more of that good wine for us."

"I did indeed, Fred," Dom said, "but I think we'd best save it for our dinner tonight."

"I'll look forward to it," Fred replied. He then pointed to a picture on the wall behind their table and said, "I just put that picture up yesterday. Could I interest you in hearing the story behind it?"

Randy & Dom grinned at Fred, and Dom replied, "It would be a great treat to hear it Fred."

Fred started, "Well, as you can see the picture is of a fellow standing in front of the offices of Dunn & Bradstreet in New York City. The picture was taken by a man from here in Harlan named Sam. As it turns out, Sam attended his Harlan High School class reunion last month, and at the reunion he got to talking with one of his old teachers, Mrs. Dunn. During the course of their conversation Sam told Mrs. Dunn that he was going to New York City the following day. Mrs. Dunn got a big grin on her face and then said, 'You know Sam, I have a son that lives in New York City .... his name is John Dunn. I haven't heard from John in a long time and I'm worried about him. Should you run into him while you're there please tell him I'm worried and would like him to call me'. He said, 'Mrs. Dunn, I certainly will'. So the following day Sam was riding in a taxi down a street in New York City when he noticed a building with the sign, 'Dunn & Bradstreet'. Sam figured this had to be where John worked, so he told the taxi driver to stop and let him out. He walked into the building and there was a nice lady sitting behind a desk in the lobby, and she said, 'May I help you sir?'. Sam said, 'Yes, do you have a John here?'. The lady got a strange look on her face and she pointed around the corner and said, 'First door on the right'. Sam started around the corner just as a man emerged from the first door on the right. Sam said to him, 'Sir, are you Dunn?'. The man looked at Sam and said, 'Yeah, and I sure feel better now!'. To which Sam said, "Well, call your mother, she's worried about you!'. Then they walked outside the building and Sam took that picture of the fellow."

Dom and Randy roared with laughter, and then Randy said, "What did Mrs. Dunn say when she saw the picture?"

Fred replied, "Well, she wasn't very pleased. She told Sam that was not John, but thanked him for his effort anyway."

•••

Back at Maggard's grocery Trigger had been putting his plan together now that he knew exactly what was going to take place on Saturday. After thinking things out for several hours he pushed the intercom button and asked Fatso if he would come back to his office.

Fatso entered Trigger's office after about 10 minutes and said, "Sorry to be so long getting back here, but I had a customer I had to take care of. Stores all clear now. What's up?"

Trigger responded, "Fatso, you know ole Tony and Max were in here this morning. They were here to go over the plans for what's going to go down on Saturday. I know I haven't told you any of the particulars of my business with them, but as we discussed earlier I'm going to need your help."

"Anything at all, Trigger," replied Fatso. "I just have a bad feeling about both of those guys. I'll be happy to have our business with them concluded."

"Ditto that," said Trigger. "I've been thinking about this and I've come up with a plan that should take care of everything. If all goes as I see it, we should never see those two again after Saturday. Here's what I need you to do. About 10 am Saturday I'll take over the grocery store for you while you run an errand for me. I want you to drive my car into town and park where you can and go to the ceremony at the Court House. The program there starts at 11 am, and I think they have several speakers. I want you to just watch and listen to the program. Tony Beekins and Max Robertson will be on the stage to speak. When Tony concludes his talk he will then leave the stage to go get some suitcases with computer parts to display.

When Tony leaves the stage you are to immediately leave, get in your car, and then drive to the old railroad yard in the subdivision called Sunshine just West of the by-pass. It's less than a mile, shouldn't take more than 10 minutes to get there. When you get there open the trunk of my car and very carefully remove the suitcase that will be in there. Place the suitcase in an open area there in the railroad yard so it's not near anywhere where people might be. Then get back in my car and start driving back here. Just as soon as you leave the Sunshine subdivision, get the little remote control box out of my glove compartment, and press the red button. You'll then see and hear a very large explosion from the suitcase you just left. When you see and hear this, you'll know that we're done with Tony and Max. Do you understand?"

Fatso replied, "I do. I think I can handle that. Should I come on back here to the store after the explosion?"

"No, don't rush," Trigger replied. "All hell will break loose when the explosion occurs. Just drive South on the by-pass on out to your old McDonalds and eat lunch. Then you can return here to the store after lunch. All should have calmed down a bit by then."

"Sounds good to me," Fatso replied. "Hey boss, you know how you fit an elephant into a matchbox?"

Trigger just stared at Fatso.

Fatso replied, "You fit an elephant into a matchbox by taking out the matches!"

Trigger continued to stare at Fatso.

Then Fatso said, "And do you know how you fit a tiger into a matchbox?"

Trigger continued his stare.

Fatso replied, "You fit a tiger into a matchbox by taking out the elephant!"

Trigger then pointed his finger toward the door. Fatso left.

• • •

Sheriff J. Bert Sterling, Harlan City Police Chief B.B. Asher, and Officer Ape Cornett with the Kentucky State Police were all gathered in Sheriff Sterling's office.

Bert began, "Chief, it's always good to see you, and Ape, it's just like old times having you back here in my office. It looks like life with the State Police is agreeing well with you."

Ape replied, "Bert, it is like a homecoming for me. I

appreciated being given this duty so I could get back here to see you and all my other friends."

"Anytime you can make it back to Harlan our door is always open to you Ape," replied Bert. "Now Chief, I understand that your people are going to take care of directing all the traffic for Saturday's event. It's my understanding that Central Street from First to Second Streets will be closed off as well as those sections of First and Second Streets that border the Court House, is that correct?"

"That's the plan," replied Chief Asher. "We're hoping to get folks to park in the Harlan Center parking lots. That plus the street parking should provide plenty of space. One of my concerns is the media parking. From what I hear we'll have quite a few television trucks in here, and my plan is to locate them on the closed streets. They'll just have to be ready to move pretty quickly after the event when we open everything back up."

Bert spoke, "Ape, the State Police are providing 10 troopers to help primarily with security. I assume most of these will be dispersed in the crowd. But I think I recall you saying that you would be on the stage. Is that correct?"

Ape said, "Correct. Also, the Governor and Secretary will be arriving by plane at the Harlan airport. I'll have a couple of cars there to gather them and bring them here to the Court House. The latest I heard is that they plan to arrive at 10 am, so it will likely be about 10:30 or so by the time we can get them here. That assumes, of course, that they are running on schedule. Politicians are not really known for that, but we'll do the best we can."

"I'm sure you will," replied Bert. "And I assume when the event is over the same two officers will take the Governor and Secretary back to the airport."

"Yes," said Ape.

Bert continued, "Now my understanding regarding the Senator is that he will be arriving by private automobile. I think he has some kind of breakfast in Corbin Saturday morning, and will leave for Harlan right after the breakfast. He should be here between 10 and 10:30 if all goes well. Chief, will you be able to park his car close to the Court House?"

"Yes, we'll park him on the street directly behind the Court House. Should not be a problem."

Bert then said, "Well guys, I think we've got our bases

covered. I sure appreciate all your assistance on this. It's certainly been a while since we've had a public event this large, and while I'm still a bit nervous about the whole thing, I think we've done about all we can do to try and make sure it comes off well. If so, Harlan County should benefit greatly from what will be announced. Be sure to convey my sincere thanks to all your people that will be involved."

All three then stood and shook hands, then Officer Cornett and Chief Asher departed.

Chapter 23

Betty Bell had been working in the kitchen cooking dinner for most of the afternoon. Her husband, Pastor Raymond Bell, got home from the New Hope Baptist Church around 5 o'clock and had joined in helping Betty prepare for the evening meal. The table would be set for 10 people. In addition to Betty and Raymond, there would be the Sheriff, Kyle and Carolyn Potter, Randy and Dom, Mayor Knapp, and Jake and Jan Keller. The Kellers had been invited because of the news that Dom was going to share about his plans for a vineyard and wine operation in Harlan County. Betty had decided on spaghetti with meat balls, a garden salad, home made bread and her special cherry pie for dessert.

Raymond and Betty were originally from Tavares, Florida. They grew up as friends and attended high school together, and started dating while in their sophomore year of high school.

The two then went to college at Florida State University in Tallahassee. Raymond majored in History, and was encouraged by his professors to continue for a Master's degree, which he did.

Raymond's mother was originally from Lexington, Kentucky, and he had visited there many times during his childhood and grew to love the Bluegrass State. After finishing at FSU Raymond and Betty were married and moved to Lexington where the two taught at Bryan Station High School. Raymond taught history and Betty taught art. After a year Raymond felt called to the ministry and enrolled at nearby Asbury Theological Seminary in Wilmore. After three years he received a Master of Theology degree. While living in Lexington, Raymond and Betty became good friends with Dr. Randy Peters. They had first met Randy when they attended a seminar he presented addressing *The History of Harlan County*. This had been the topic of Randy's Ph.D. dissertation and he was intimately familiar with Eastern Kentucky in general, and Harlan County in particular. He had invited Raymond and Betty to accompany him on several research related trips to Harlan, and they too had fallen in love with Harlan and its people. So after completing school at Asbury the two jumped at the chance for Raymond to apply for pastor at New Hope Baptist Church when their pastor retired. The church extended the call to Raymond, and he and Betty had been lovingly embraced by not only the church but by the entire community ever since.

At 6:15 Betty proclaimed dinner was all set and she ran upstairs to get herself properly dressed for the evening. Raymond was left to meet and greet the guests as they arrived.

By 6:45 all the guests were present and accounted for, and Betty had returned to the kitchen. All the ladies were helping Betty, and the men sat in the living room doing the chit-chat waiting for the call to dinner. It came promptly at 7 pm.

Everyone gathered around the table, held hands, and had their gathering and the food properly blessed by Pastor Bell. They then sat and began their meal.

Dom said, "Betty, I feel the fact that we're enjoying your delicious spaghetti and meat balls might somehow relate to my being here and being Italian!"

Betty replied, "I must admit that I did ponder for a while trying to think what to have. And I guess the spaghetti and meat balls just seemed appropriate. I hope you approve."

"Indeed I do. It's superb," said Dom. "And if you will allow me, I brought a few bottles of my wine that I thought might go with our dinner."

Betty responded, "That would just top it off perfectly, Dom. Thank you."

Dom then opened two bottles of his Pelle wine and filled everyone's glass.

Raymond then said, "Certainly as a rule Betty and I abstain from alcohol. But on special occasions such as the one tonight we allow ourselves to enjoy a glass of wine with friends, as did our Lord Jesus Christ. So I would propose a toast." And Raymond raised his glass and said, "To our new Italian friend Dom, and to all our wonderful old friends. Thank you for joining Betty and me this evening!"

After the wonderful meal the group moved to the living room.

Bert began, "Such a wonderful meal. I know I speak for all your guests here this evening when I thank you for the great job in preparing the meal, it could not have been better. And that cherry pie was the perfect finishing touch."

Raymond responded, "Betty and I enjoyed greatly being able to prepare and serve the meal. You honor us by your presence."

Bert continued, "I guess it would now be appropriate to talk a little business. Why don't we begin with Dom and the wine. I know the Kellers must be anxious to hear about this."

Dom responded, "Be happy to. I think everyone is aware that during my visit with the Kellers last week I was tremendously impressed by the quality of their wine. And for that I owe a big thank you to Kyle Potter for bringing it to my attention, and to the Kellers for allowing me to see their vineyard and sample their wine. Jake allowed me to take a bottle to send to my laboratory in Prato for analysis, and the results from that were most encouraging. Amazingly to me, the Keller wine compares very favorably to my Pelle wine. As soon as I got this great news I asked a couple of my people to travel immediately to Harlan County to start looking for appropriate land for a vineyard. It is my intention to purchase such land and start growing grapes. If all goes as anticipated, in just a few years Pelle will have a wine producing operation here in Harlan County to equal that in Prato. And Jake, I realize you are no 'spring chicken' as you Americans like to say, but I would like you to consider taking on the responsibility for developing my Harlan County vineyard. Certainly you are the only person in Harlan County with the experience and know-how to accomplish what I want. You did it on your property on a small scale, and now I'd like that expanded on my new Harlan County property. You don't have to give me an answer tonight, I just wanted to make you the offer. You would be very handsomely compensated....equal to what I pay those directing my Prato operation. If you would do me the favor of considering my offer, I'll have paperwork drawn up and present it to you in the next few days. It would be my contention that this represents the start of Harlan County's wine production, and that a few years from now it will represent a significant portion of Harlan County's economy. Will you consider it?"

"I just hardly know what to say, Dom," replied Jake.

"Never in my wildest dreams would I have thought that my little vineyard and wine making would be such a catalyst. Yes, I'll be more than happy to talk with Jan about your most generous and gracious offer, but I'll tell you right up front that I feel like we will definitely be working together."

Bert then said, "Okay, so much for the wine thing! And just to make sure we have our ducks in a row, Dom you will be making all this public at the Saturday ceremony?"

"That's my plan," Dom responded. "The two guys from my Prato operation arrived here in Harlan on Tuesday, and they have located a 100 acre piece of property that would seem ideal for our operation. The land is located not far from Wallins and includes a good frontage on the Cumberland River and good rolling hills for the vineyard. I've already contacted the owner of the property and we have signed a contract. Closing is set for early next week. So I'm prepared to make all this public knowledge on Saturday."

Fred spoke up, "Boy oh boy, that will really be well received. I'm sure the governor and his economic development secretary will turn flips over that news. And there will be a huge number of people here in Harlan County that will start reading up on growing grapes!"

"I think you're right Mr. Mayor," Bert replied. "So now what about the Pelle Anchor Cross announcement and showing?"

Randy spoke up, "Got it right here." And he pulled the Pelle Anchor Cross from under his sweater and took it's necklace from around his neck and passed it among the group for gawking. "I'll talk a bit about it's origin and relationship to the Seibert Anchor Cross, and then I'll simply hold the cross so that those in the audience can get a good look and take pictures. I really do not intend to let it out of my possession, and I feel much safer knowing that Officer Potter and Officer Cornett will be close by for protection."

"I'll be right there," Kyle responded.

Pastor Raymond Bell was holding and closely inspecting the Pelle Anchor Cross. Tears appeared to be forming in his eyes as he said, "This is just so remarkable. To believe that the gold in this cross I'm holding was once before the face of our Lord Jesus Christ, and received his blessing! And I now hold it in my hand. I am humbled and greatly honored to be able to view and hold this precious anchor cross."

Randy then said, "I feel your emotion Raymond. And I understand. The thing too that makes these Savior's Crosses so unique is that they represent the very first time in history that the cross was used to symbolize Christianity. These Savior's Crosses were made by Constantine the Great around 325 AD, after his conversion to Christianity. Prior to that time the cross was a symbol associated with the very worst of criminals. Only they were crucified. So from before the time of Christ until the time of Constantine the anchor was the primary religious symbol. As Hebrews 6:19 says, *'We have this hope as an anchor for the soul, firm and secure'*. So in the anchor cross Constantine combined these two symbols, and from that time forward the cross has become the primary Christian symbol, representing the death, and then resurrection, of our Lord Jesus Christ."

Bert then said, "Well, it certainly has been a full day. And this evening will long be fondly remembered. But all good things must come to an end, so I suggest we now call it a day and depart from our gracious hosts."

After many handshakes, hugs, and kisses the group departed and went their respective ways.

Chapter 24

Dom and Randy were staying at the Holiday Inn Express in Harlan. They had been invited by several of their Harlan friends to stay with them, but declined in order to have time at the motel to do business via telephone and computer.

Friday morning around 9 am Dom got a phone call in his room from Jake Keller telling him that he had discussed Dom's offer with his wife Jan and they enthusiastically accepted. They then agreed to get together at 1 pm at the Keller's home to further discuss the development of the new Harlan vineyard. Dom phoned Randy's room to ask if he would like to accompany him to the Kellers. Randy said he would, that he had finished all the work that he could do from the motel. He then asked Dom if he would like to have lunch prior to their going to the Kellers. Dom agreed, and they met in the motel lobby at 11:30.

Randy said, "Morning Dom, got any preference for lunch?"

"Hey, you know Harlan a lot better than I do .... you pick it," replied Dom.

"Well, there's a great little Mexican restaurant not far from here, does that sound okay?" asked Randy.

"That'll work," answered Dom.

The two got into Randy's car and started driving along the by-pass.

Randy commented, "Dom, in my research I discovered that Harlan once had 5 drive-in restaurants. I'm talking about the kind prominent back in the 50s and 60s. Here in Kentucky a lot of people called them 'custard stands', because they all served a soft ice cream made and dispensed in the restaurant. They had hot dogs, hamburgers, thick milk shakes, root beer in frozen mugs, and lots of other sandwiches and drinks. These were all locally owned, there were no franchise restaurants then. There on your right we're passing what was the location of one of those drive-ins, it was called Jacks. The other four in and around Harlan were Denny Rays, Mikes, Dixie, and Jays. Nothing left of those now except the memories. Did you have anything like that in Italy?"

"No, I guess that was an American thing," replied Dom. "But it sounds good."

"Yeah, it sure was."

"One other thing about those drive-in restaurants," Randy commented. "I heard that after the fifth one was built someone said they were going to build one more in Harlan and call it 'Custard's Last Stand' ...... a little play on words! But that one didn't develop!"

With that they arrived at the Mexican restaurant for lunch.

Promptly at 1 pm they arrived at the Keller home, and knocked on the door. Jan greeted them and invited them in. Jake joined the other three and they all took a seat in the living room.

Dom said, "Jan, Jake, I am just really excited that you two are going to direct the development of my vineyard here in Harlan County. When I leave I will do so knowing that everything is in good hands. I know that you two know how to grow the kind of grapes that we need, so thanks again for accepting the responsibility."

Jake replied, "Dom it will truly be an honor to attempt to get your Harlan County operation underway. Jan and I will do our best, that's about all we can promise."

The four spent the next couple of hours going over details and paperwork, and then they spent another hour or so walking outside looking over the Keller vineyard again.

At 4:30 Dom said, "Well folks, unless you have additional questions Randy and I probably should be headed back to town. We have a little preparation to do for the big day tomorrow. We'll look forward to seeing you two at the Court House."

They all said good-byes, and Randy and Dom headed back to Harlan.

• • •

Friday morning around 8 am Trigger was finishing his morning coffee at his home. Max, as usual, was still sleeping. Trigger needed to talk with Max before he left for the grocery store, so he knocked on Max's bedroom door and said, "Hey Max, I need to chat with you a minute before I go to work ..... can you pop up?"

A sleepy Max shouted to the closed door, "Give me a minute and I'll be out."

After a few minutes Max walked into Tirgger's kitchen wearing a T-shirt and jeans. He said, "What'd you want to talk about?"

Trigger replied, "I wanted to talk about tomorrow. The main thing I'm concerned with is that explosive suit in the trunk of your car. I know you will be wearing it tomorrow, so I was afraid that you might elect to bring it into my house sometime today or tonight so you would have it handy to put on in the morning. I do not want you to do that. I know you have to bring it in here sometime, but I want that sometime to be tomorrow morning after I've left for work. I'm really concerned that the explosives could detonate unexpectedly and blow up my house and everything and everyone in it. I'll chance losing my house, I figure that's part of my deal with Tony, but I won't chance losing my life. So I don't want that thing in my home while I'm here. After I leave in the morning you can get it out of the trunk of your car and bring it in. Not before that. Do you understand?"

"I understand," replied Max.

Trigger continued, "I may not get a chance to talk with you again before you go on your mission tomorrow, so just let me say that I hope all goes as you intend, and that Allah receives you as you expect him to."

Max said, "Thank you."

With that Trigger left his home for the grocery store. Max returned to bed.

•••

Sheriff Sterling walked into Creech Cafe about mid afternoon. Fred was on his cell phone sitting at a table in the back. After greeting Polly in the appropriate fashion, he walked back and had a seat at the table with Fred.

Fred finished his conversation and said, "Bert, good to see you. Anything new?"

Bert replied, "Quiet.....almost too quiet, Fred. But I guess I shouldn't complain. As far as I know everything is going well. Who you talking to on the phone?"

"You sure are nosy," Fred replied.

"I'm the sheriff. I can be nosy," answered Bert.

"I guess," said Fred. "Actually that was the Governor's appointments secretary I was talking with. She was just checking to see if we had our ducks in a row for tomorrow. She actually said the Governor was excited about the whole thing and that he was looking forward to his Harlan visit. Just before I talked with her I had a call from the Senator's office asking about the same thing. So I guess everything is good to go at 11 am tomorrow. Any problems develop from your end?"

Bert said, "Not that I'm aware of. I guess we all need to just get a real good night's rest and be all ready for a full day tomorrow."

"I plan to go home shortly, grab a sandwich, watch the evening news, and then hit the sack," replied the Mayor. "But just before we call it quits for the day, I was talking with a customer a moment ago and he told me a good one .... are you up to it?"

"Yeah, it may help me sleep. Go right ahead Fred," Bert replied.

Fred said, "This customer said people in Harlan County were getting all excited about the rumor of a new manufacturing plant coming to town. He said it reminded him of the story about the Fruit of the Loom plant in Kentucky that was manufacturing men's underwear. He said the plant packaged the underwear in packages of 7 for everywhere other than Kentucky. One pair for Monday, one for Tuesday, one for Wednesday, etc. But for their customers in Kentucky they packaged the underwear in packages of 12. One for January, one for February, one for March. etc."

Bert said, "Yeah, that'll help me sleep. See you tomorrow Mr. Mayor."

Chapter 25

Saturday, October 10th had arrived. It was 3 am in the morning, and Trigger Green was moving through his own home like a burglar! All the lights were off in his house, and he moved with the aid of a flashlight from his bedroom toward the living room, being extra quiet in order to not wake Max. He got to the front door, twisted the knob, slowly opened the door and walked outside.

Trigger was far from the best of students when he attended Harlan High School, but he did manage to graduate. He was far from stupid, just not very motivated. After graduation he did like so many other kids in the county, he enlisted in the Army. While in the army he was assigned to a unit that specialized in explosives. After spending most of his enlistment working with various kinds of bombs, he became quite familiar with handling and wiring them. Tonight that training would serve him well.

Trigger demanded that Max park his car well away from his home. If the explosives in the suicide suit accidently detonated he wanted the explosion to be away from his home. So Max's car was parked at the very end of Trigger's driveway. The bedroom where Max was sleeping was a back bedroom without windows that faced the front of the house. So Max could not see his car from his bedroom windows.

Trigger walked to Max's car and opened the driver's door with the key that he had removed from the living room table. He told Max to always leave the key to his car on that table in case he needed to move the car for any reason. Max had always done so. Once inside the car Trigger pushed the trunk- release button and walked around to the back of the car and opened the trunk. There in the trunk was the suitcase that contained Max's explosive suit. Trigger then walked over to his car and opened its trunk and removed a suitcase and carried it to Max's car. He placed his suitcase beside the one belonging to Max, and then opened his. Inside there were 7 rectangular brick-like blocks. Each had a thin, white plastic cover. Trigger then carefully opened Max's suitcase. Inside was the explosive suit that Max would wear to the ceremony later today. He carefully removed the suit jacket, turned it inside out, and spread it across the suitcase. On the inside of the jacket there were three pockets, and inside each was a brick of plastic C-4 explosive. The jacket also contained the detonator. Trigger recognized the electronic detonator to be one that he had worked with in the army. The detonator was wired to the C-4 explosive block that was fitted into the pocket in the back of the jacket. There were also similar blocks of C-4 in pockets on each side of the jacket and two in each leg of the suit pants. There were a total of 7 blocks of C-4 in the suit. The previous evening Trigger had followed the exact routine he was following tonight just to examine the explosive suit to determine the number and size of the explosive blocks. During the day yesterday he constructed 7 identical blocks that contained sand wrapped with a thin white plastic wrap. These weighed just about the same as the explosive blocks, and would pass a quick inspection.

He already had a detonator identical to the one he found in the explosive suit.

Next he very carefully removed the detonator from the jacket. On one end of the detonator was a small device called a logger. The other end ran to the block of C-4 in the back of the suit jacket. The logger was a programmable device that determined the amount of time from initiation to detonation. It could be set in milliseconds from 1 to 10,000. Trigger had noticed that it was set for 1 millisecond. A string about 18 inches long was attached to the logger. When the suit jacket was worn the string was looped over the left shoulder and hung loose on the front inside of the jacket. When it was desired to detonate the bomb the person wearing the jacket would reach his right hand inside the left front part of the jacket, grab the string, and pull. When he did this the other end of the string would pull the switch on the end of the logger that would in one millisecond trigger the detonator attached to the explosive block of C-4. The force of the explosion of this one block would then immediately trigger the other 6 blocks. This was enough C-4 to bring down a sizeable building.

After removing the detonator, Trigger then gingerly

removed each of the 7 blocks of C-4. All of these, including the detonator, he placed in one side of his suitcase. From the other side of his suitcase he removed the 7 sand-filled blocks and placed them in the suit pockets, then he got the detonator that he had constructed identical to the one in the suit and wired it. When finished Max's suit looked exactly the same as before, but now all the explosives were replaced with blocks of sand.

Trigger then carefully arranged the blocks of C-4 in his suitcase. He then walked back to his car, reached into the trunk and retrieved a small box and brought it back to Max's car. He carefully placed this box inside his suitcase beside the blocks of C-4 and then closed the suitcase. He carried the suitcase back to his car and placed it gently into the trunk. He closed the trunk, walked back to Max's car, refolded Max's suit, and placed it back in Max's suitcase and closed it. He then closed the trunk of Max's car.

The box that Trigger had placed inside the suitcase with the C-4 that was now in the trunk of his car contained a small brick of explosive fitted with an electronic detonator that was activated by a remote control box that he had placed in the glove compartment of his car. It was the red button on this remote control that Fatso would push to detonate all the explosives.

The mission was accomplished. Trigger then walked back into his house, replaced Max's car keys on the living room table, and headed for bed.

•••

At 7 am Trigger awoke. After a trip to the bathroom, he headed for the kitchen to make coffee. As he was making the coffee and fixing some toast he glanced into his living room and was startled to see Max sitting there in his T-shirt and jeans just staring into space.

"Morning Max," Trigger said.

"Good morning Trigger," Max replied.

"I'm making coffee and toast, would you like some?" asked Trigger

"That would be good," Max replied.

After the coffee and toast were ready, Trigger brought them on plates to the living room and handed one to Max.

Max said, "Thank you."

Trigger replied, "No problem. So I guess the big day is

here. If all goes as planned you'll meet Allah and all those virgins later today and I'll meet my $250,000 payment!"

"Yes," replied Max.

The two then sat quietly and finished their coffee and toast. Trigger then excused himself to get ready for work. After another 20 minutes Trigger walked back into the living room on his way out of the house. Max was still sitting in the chair staring at space.

Trigger said, "Well ole buddy, been good knowing you. Give my regards to Allah." And he shook hands with Max.

"I'm out of here. Got work to do. Be very careful when you bring that explosive suit into my house. I'd really appreciate it if my house was still standing when I get back home," Trigger said.

"Yes," replied Max.

Trigger then walked to his car and left for the grocery store.

As soon as Trigger was gone Max grabbed his car keys from the living room table and walked to his car, opened the driver's door and pushed the trunk-release button. He then walked to the back of his car, opened the trunk, and carefully removed the suitcase. After closing the trunk he then carried the suitcase into the house. It was time to get dressed.

•••

Trigger arrived at the grocery store, parked in front, and then walked into the store. Fatso was at the cash register and said, "Hey Trigger, good morning! You know why the elephant fell out of the tree?"

Trigger just stared at Fatso.

"The elephant fell out of the tree because he was dead!" Fatso replied with a giggle.

Trigger said, "I'm heading back to my office. At 10 am I'll come back out here to relieve you so you can drive my car into town on that little errand we talked about. Do you have any questions?"

Fatso replied, "Hey Boss, I'm all set. Just looking forward to having all this over with so we won't be seeing Tony and Max anymore."

Trigger replied, "Yeah, me too ..... believe me!"

Fatso pressed the button to open the door to Trigger's office. Trigger entered, walked over to the coffee machine and made coffee, and then sat down at his desk. He thought, just a few more hours and all this nightmare should be over!

Chapter 26

Mayor Fred Knapp looked at his watch. 7 am. It already looked like a zoo out here by the Harlan County Court House. Television satellite trucks had been arriving for over an hour. They were all being parked on First Street beside the Court House. This portion of the street had been closed off to traffic by the Harlan City Police since 5 am. There were satellite trucks from Louisville, Huntington, Knoxville, and Lexington. The latter was from the CBS affiliate WKYT, and Harlan native and television anchor Barbara Clark was standing beside their truck. When Fred spotted Barbara he hurried over to her.

"Top of the morning Ms. Clark," Fred offered. "You're here for an early start I see."

Barbara responded, "Hi Mr. Mayor. So good to see you again. Yes, everyone is all excited about the upcoming ceremony. It promises to offer all those good newsworthy topics. New jobs for the unemployed, the unveiling of a mysterious new golden anchor cross, and I even hear rumors of some new type of industry for the county. I sure didn't want to miss this. And being from Harlan just makes it all very special to me."

"Well, I can tell you that as Mayor of our fair town I'm equally excited. I just can hardly contain myself until 11 am. Please let me know if there's anything at all I can do to be of assistance to you. Of course I love all the media folks, but you are truly special .... being a Harlan native and all," Fred replied.

"Thanks Mr. Mayor, I sure will," Barbara responded.

Fred looked around and saw two food trucks parked on the closed portion of Second Street that bordered the Court House. Folks in these trucks were currently serving a lot of coffee and doughnuts. The City Police had also directed several other State Police cruisers to park there, and Fred also saw a couple of cars there with signs in the windshield that read 'Press'. No doubt about it, it was going to be a media event of the first magnitude. Even some of the audience had already started to arrive with folding chairs, and lined these up in a row close to the stage. These folks were now just milling about talking with anyone they ran into. Several county employees were busy setting up the sound system, including microphones and loud speakers. A podium was prominently positioned at the center of the stage and out near its edge. As you faced the stage there were six chairs positioned to the left of the podium, and six to its right. These 12 chairs would soon be filled by the Mayor, the Sheriff, Deputy Potter, Officer Cornett, Randy Peters, Dom Pelle, Jake Keller, Tony Beekins, Max Robertson, Governor Brad Shear, Secretary Helen O'Malley, and Senator Rich McDonald. There were even several vendors set up with tables selling everything from coal jewelry to books related to Harlan County. Fred noticed one such table that had several stacks of books written by two graduates of Harlan High School; Bill J. Looney and Richard G. Edwards. Yeah, it was a circus.

One big worry that concerned Fred about the event

was the weather. But apparently someone had paid the preacher .... the weather weenies said today should be a gorgeous fall day. Temperatures were predicted to rise to a balmy 75 degrees by noon, and the chance of rain was nil. Couldn't have ordered up any better weather.

Around 8 am Fred walked back to his cafe and walked in. "Hey Freddie, Hey Freddie," Polly greeted.

"Morning Bird," Fred said as he gave Polly a stroke. He then walked in back of the counter, spoke to his employees, and gathered a cup of coffee. Just as he was about to have a seat at a table the Sheriff walked in. "The Law's here. The Law's here," squawked Polly.

Bert walked over and sat with Fred and said, "Looks like you got everything under control Fred."

So far, so good," replied the Mayor. "Probably not much going to happen between now and about 10 o'clock. I figure the speakers will start to show up then and the audience will have grown considerable. From 10 to noon is my big concern."

"That's likely correct," replied Bert. "But I still feel confident that everything will come off smoothly. I think we've got all our bases covered."

"I sure hope so," responded Fred. "But I still like to worry about it!"

Bert replied, "That I know."

Polly decided she needed a little exercise so she flew over to Fred and landed on his shoulder. "Love Freddie, Love Freddie," she said.

"Quit trying to butter me up, Bird," replied Fred. Then Fred thought for a moment and said, "Ole Polly here does remind me of a story I heard yesterday Bert .... you up to it?"

Bert replied, "Sure, we got a little time."

Fred said, "This guy went to a pet store and bought a parrot. The guy at the pet store guaranteed that the bird would talk. After about a week the guy that bought the parrot came back in the pet store and said 'I've tried all week to get my bird to talk, and he won't say a word'. The pet store guy said 'That sometimes happens. You need to get a file and file off just a little of his beak. That should get him talking'. The next day the guy with the parrot walks back in the pet store and says 'My parrot's dead'. Pet store guy says 'Dead? Did you file off too much of his beak?'. Parrot owner said 'No, no, it couldn't have been that ... he was dead when I took him out of the vise!'

Bert grinned and looked at Polly and said, "You better keep talking Polly."

Bert then stood and told Fred, "I'm going back over to my office. I'll see you shortly for the ceremony."

•••

Shortly after 10 Randy, Dom, and Deputy Kyle Potter walked into the Sheriff's office. Each spoke to Preacher Puss and gave her a gentle stroke. She swished her tail and started her motor running loudly .... she loved attention.

Rosie said, "Good morning all. Glad to see you made it safely here."

"Morning Rosie," Randy replied. "Since Deputy Potter insisted on picking us up at the motel and giving us an armed escort we could be nothing but safe!"

"You're in good hands with Kyle," she replied.

Dom said, "We are indeed. Is Bert in his office?"

"Yep, please just go right in. He's expecting you. Could I get you some coffee?" she asked.

"I think we're all fine .... had a good breakfast, but thanks anyway," Randy replied as they entered the Sheriff's office.

After greeting the Sheriff the three took seats and chatted, awaiting the arrival of Jake Keller. No more than 5 minutes passed before Jake entered the office and greeted everyone.

The sheriff then said, "Well, I think everyone that was coming here to my office has now arrived. I'm sure the Mayor will be on the lookout for the politicians, and Tony Beekins and Max Robertson were told to be here no later than 10:30, but I guess we'll just meet them outside when they show up. You all ready to move along?"

All nodded in agreement, stood, and exited the sheriff's office.

•••

It was now 10:30 am. The crowd had grown to the point where the entire lawn of the Court House was full of people, spilling over into Central Street, which had been closed. The television people had brought portable stands upon which they stood with their television cameras. One row of seats in the front of the audience had been roped off for the press, and there appeared to be about 10 of those chairs taken. The excitement was growing.

Fred was standing beside the stairs going up to the stage. He was awaiting the arrival of the Governor and Senator. As he scanned the crowd he saw Fatso Chapel standing in the middle of Central Street in front of Creech Cafe. Odd he thought. Fatso normally stays pretty close to Maggard's grocery. Guess the big hype got even Fatso out.

The Mayor then heard the sirens. He turned to his right to see two state police cars with a black Suburban sandwiched between them. The Harlan City Police directed them to their designated parking behind the Court House. Fred then saw the doors open on the Suburban and Senator Rich McDonald emerge with a couple of his aids. About the same time the doors on the State Police car in the back of the Suburban opened and both the Governor and the Secretary got out along with Officer Ape Cornett. The entire group then started walking around the side of the Court House headed toward the front and the steps where Fred stood.

With a giant grin on his face Fred extended his hand

and said, "Governor, Madame Secretary, I'm Mayor Fred Knapp. Welcome to Harlan!"

Governor Shear gave a big grin back to Fred, and while shaking his hand said, "Mayor, it's a pleasure for us to be here. Thank you so much for putting all this together."

Secretary Helen O'Malley then said, "And are you also responsible for this great weather?"

"I'll gladly take credit Ms. O'Malley," the Mayor responded. He then extended his hand to Senator McDonald who was walking behind and said, "Senator this is a great day for Harlan and for Kentucky. We really appreciate your being here to help us today."

Senator McDonald responded with a hearty handshake and said, "Mayor Knapp the pleasure is all mine. Harlan is one of my favorite towns, and the news that we bring today should be extremely well received. I too thank you for all your assistance."

With that the delegation started to climb the stairs to the stage. State Trooper Ape Cornett followed behind the Senator. Fred shook his hand and slapped him on his back and said, "Ape, always good to have you back here in Harlan."

Ape replied, "I feel like I'm back home Fred."

The Sheriff, Randy, Dom, Kyle, and Jake were already on the stage standing beside their seats. As the politicians passed they all shook hands and exchanged a few words. The politicians then proceeded to their chairs and stood. Trooper Cornett and Mayor Knapp then took their place.

Two seats remained unfilled. The mayor walked over to the Sheriff and asked, "Bert, Beekins and Robertson are not here. Have you seen them this morning?"

"I have not, Mayor," replied Bert. "Must have gotten held up in traffic. We'll wait a few minutes to see if they show. If they don't arrive in the next 5 minutes perhaps I'll make a phone call to try and locate them."

"I told them to be here by 10:30," Mayor Knapp replied.

Just then Bert saw the two making their way through the crowd.

"Over there Mayor," Bert said as he pointed toward them.

"Ah, I feel better," Fred replied.

Tony and Max climbed the steps to the stage and started shaking hands with everyone. Tony said they got in some heavy traffic and apologized to all for being late. When they were finished they took their places standing in front of their seats. At that moment applause broke out from the crowd. It grew to a great din. The gathered crowd was ready for the ceremony to begin. The television cameras were rolling and the press was snapping photographs as quickly as they could trigger their shutters.

All those on the stage started waving to the crowd. They then took their seats, and Mayor Knapp walked to the podium. The ceremony was ready to begin.

Chapter 27

The applause continued as Mayor Knapp stood at the podium. He then motioned with palms down on both hands asking for quiet. The applause stopped.

The Mayor began, "Good morning ladies and gentlemen, Governor Shear, Secretary O'Malley, Senator McDonald, my other good friends on the stage, and all those watching today on television. My name is Fred Knapp, the Mayor of Harlan. It is indeed a great day for Harlan and Harlan County. Shortly you will hear announcements that will profoundly change the economy of our town and county. In addition, a beautiful golden anchor cross will be displayed that has, like the one discovered here in Harlan County twelve years ago, found its way to our city. So let us begin. I would now like to introduce to you all the folks that have joined me and are seated here on the platform. Going from left to right we have Deputy Sheriff Kyle Potter, Sheriff J. Bert Sterling, Mr. Domenico Pelle, Dr. Randy Peters, Mr. Max Robertson, Mr. Anthony Beekins, Senator Rich McDonald, Governor Brad Shear, Economic Development Secretary Helen O'Malley, my empty seat, Mr. Jake Keller, and last, but certainly not least, Trooper Ape Cornett."

There was a nice round of applause.

Fred continued, "So first I would like to call Governor Shear to the podium. Ladies and gentlemen, the governor of the commonwealth of Kentucky, Brad Shear."

The governor stood and walked to the podium and waved as the audience applauded him. He then began a speech that lasted about 15 minutes in which he said he was greatly excited about the upcoming announcements, and that he felt the economy of Harlan County would benefit greatly from the two announcements that would soon be made. He then thanked everyone for their presence, and the Mayor for making the event possible. Before he concluded he introduced Helen O'Malley.

She then came to the podium and made complimentary remarks similar to those of the governor, and concluded by saying that she was especially delighted to learn of the upcoming developments that would contribute greatly to the county's economy.

Mayor Knapp then stood at the podium and thanked the governor and secretary for their comments, and then introduced Senator McDonald.

The senator waved wildly to the audience for several minutes during his applause, and then started his talk, "My friends I come to Harlan County today to announce a new manufacturing plant that will be built here and will employ over 50 of our citizens. The name of the new plant will be AB Enterprises. It will manufacture computer parts, similar to one currently operating in Mexico. The owner of both the plant in Mexico and the one to be built here is Mr. Anthony Beekins. We have Mr. Beekins as well as the new plant manager, Mr. Max Robertson, here with us today. So let me now call on Mr. Anthony Beekins to give you a little more information. Anthony, the people of Harlan County are among the hardest working and most devoted workforce available anywhere. They welcome with open arms your plans to locate here in our county. Please come now and tell us a bit more about your operation. Ladies and gentlemen, Mr. Anthony Beekins."

A tremendous burst of applause erupted for Tony as he walked to the podium. After it subsided he said, "Thank you. Thank you. Thank you Senator McDonald, and thanks to you good folks of Harlan County. I feel that my company has indeed made the correct choice in locating our new plant here. We did a lot of research before deciding on Harlan County, but as the Senator said the workforce here appears to be an exact match for us. The location that we have selected is one that has road frontage on highway 119 near the town of Wallins. The property is owned by Mr. Trigger Green. He currently operates Maggard's grocery store on the property, but has over 4 acres of adjacent land that is currently vacant, and it is on that land that we will break ground for our new plant next month. The plant will be manufacturing a wide variety of computer related parts. I currently have a similar plant in Mexico that produces many of the same parts that we will be making here in Harlan County. As a matter of fact, I brought a couple of suitcases full of these parts to show you after our ceremony today. So at the conclusion of my remarks, I will excuse myself to retrieve those suitcases and bring them here to the platform and put them on display. As the Senator said, our plans call for hiring around 50 people to work in our operation. The **Harlan Daily Enterprise** will have an announcement one day next week that will contain details of these jobs and the procedure for applying for them. I will now say that a requirement for all the jobs will be that you must currently be a citizen of Harlan County. We want to help you in your struggle out of economic depression, and I feel certain we'll be able to make a good contribution."

Another great outburst of applause followed these remarks.

Tony then said, "I know we have lots of other important matters on today's agenda, so I will conclude. But before I do, I wanted to introduce you to the new AB Enterprises plant manager here in Harlan. His name is Max Robertson. Max has trained several years at my plant in Mexico. He is a native of South Africa. Max is extremely well qualified to direct the new plant. He has a superior knowledge of the manufacturing process. Unfortunately, his English is limited. So he will not be speaking today, but you'll have a good chance to get to know him in the future. I'll just ask Max now to stand, and we can give him a good welcome."

Again, a large roar of applause came from the crowd as Max stood. His bulgy suit, puffy face, and bad wig did not go together to make the best impression, and he also seemed to be sweating, but to the people of Harlan he was a new friend. Max was most welcome.

The mayor then returned to the podium, and Tony walked off the platform to retrieve the suitcases with computer parts. Just as Fred was about to introduce Dom Pelle he saw movement in the audience on Central Street. It looked like Fatso Chapel was trying to move through the crowd. He wondered what that was all about. Maybe he had to go to the bathroom! Fred then thanked both Tony and Max, and then began introducing Dom, "Ladies and Gentlemen, our next speaker undoubtedly gets the award for coming the greatest distance for today's ceremony! Domenico Pelle lives in Prato, Italy. He is the owner of the large Pelle wine operation there that has developed in his family for generations. Mr. Pelle was visited by Dr. Randy Peters a couple of weeks ago. Dr. Peters will talk about that after Mr. Pelle's comments. So please now welcome our friend from Italy, Mr. Dom Pelle."

Dom walked to the podium as the crowd gave yet another round of applause.

Dom said, "I am honored by your warm response. I have only known of Harlan for a couple of weeks, but during that time I have certainly become very fond of the city, the county, and all the people here that I've had the opportunity to meet. And I bring you greetings from my home town of Prato, Italy, where my family has been involved in growing grapes and producing wine for many generations. My coming to your country originally had nothing to do with my business, but I'll let Dr. Randy Peters talk about that later. But while I was visiting here in Harlan I was introduced to the Keller family. Jake and Jan Keller live near Wallins where they have a small farm. Among other things, they grow grapes. They have a very nice little vineyard that they have nurtured for years and it produces grapes that they use to make wine for their family and friends. In my visit to their home they invited me to take a look at their vineyard, and they allowed me to sample their wine. When I did I was very much surprised.

Their wine tasted much like my own Pelle wine. I then asked them if I could have a bottle of their wine to send to my laboratory for testing. They agreed, and after I got the results my suspicions were confirmed. The quality of their wine was near that of my own. I then became very interested in developing a vineyard and wine production operation here in Harlan County. I had a couple of my people come here and look for suitable land. I am here to announce today that Pelle wine has purchased 100 acres of Harlan County land and will begin immediately to start a vineyard that will produce the high quality grapes required for Pelle wine. Jake Keller has agreed to manage my Harlan County operation. Jake, please stand and wave at the crowd."

Jake Keller stood to a large wave of applause and then took his seat.

Dom continued, "While I am extremely pleased about the potential for my new Harlan County Pelle wine operation, I am equally excited about the potential for the development of additional vineyards and wine production in Harlan County. I think this represents a great possible new industry for the county, and I would invite anyone interested to contact me and I'll provide you additional information. Just let Mayor Knapp know of your interest and he'll pass that along to me and I'll have my people provide you all the current relevant know-how. I would welcome the competition. Thank you so much for your hospitality. I look forward greatly to meeting many of you and to spending a great deal of time in Harlan County."

Dom then took his seat as the crowd applauded. Mayor Knapp walked again to the podium and said, "Dom, my friend, thanks so much for your investment in our county. We are humbled that you have found our land to be suitable for growing quality grapes, and appreciate so much your encouragement to develop this industry. Such a suggestion coming from most people might not be well received, but coming from an authority such as you, with generations of successful wine production to your credit, I know will make people give your words careful attention. And now I want to invite my good friend Dr. Randy Peters to the podium. Most of you know Randy. He is Director of the University of Kentucky's Center for Appalachian Studies, and likely the foremost authority on the history and people of Harlan County. He was involved in the events of 12 years ago when the Seibert Anchor Cross was discovered here, and his research traced it back to the time of Christ. He comes today to tell us about another astounding anchor cross. Please welcome our friend, Dr. Randy Peters."

The crowd seemed to move as one closer to the platform. They applauded Randy as he approached the podium. When there he said, "Good morning my friends. And thanks Mr. Mayor for your kind words. It is always a privilege and honor for me to be in Harlan. I know most of you recall the events of 12 years ago when the Seibert Anchor Cross was discovered in Harlan County by Kyle Potter. As you will also recall, the Seibert Anchor Cross was later given by Kyle to my Center for Appalachian Research and it remains there today. My research had traced the Seibert Anchor Cross back to being cast by Constantine the Great around 325 AD from gold he received from Pope Sylvester I that had been blessed by Christ and then given to St. Peter to help start the church. I also discovered that Constantine made not one, but six of these beautiful golden anchor crosses. They later became known as the Savior's Crosses. Until just a couple of weeks ago I had been unsuccessful in locating any other of these crosses. Then a colleague told me about seeing one in a church in Prato, Italy that looked identical to the Seibert Anchor Cross. I then traveled to Prato and located the cross on display in the Santa Maria delle Carceri. A father Giovanni Territo allowed me to examine the cross, and then explained to me that it had been placed in his church by Domenico Pelle, who had owned the cross for generations. Father Territo contacted Dom and we all met. I told them my experience with the Seibert Anchor Cross and that I thought this cross, which we began calling the Pelle Anchor Cross, was likely also one of the Savior's Crosses. Dom and Father Territo then agreed that I could bring the Pelle Anchor Cross to my Center in Lexington for further study and analysis to establish if it was in fact one of the Savior's Crosses. Because Dom was so interested, he agreed to accompany me home and visit a few days. We decided the best way to transport the Pelle Anchor Cross safely on the trip was for me to wear it on a necklace around my neck and under my sweater. Dom and I were on that now famous Delta flight from Rome to Atlanta that barely avoided crashing. The pilot and copilot were apparently miraculously stricken with simultaneous heart attacks, and when they somehow recovered in time to avoid the crash I felt the Pelle Anchor Cross being very warm. I remind you that this was very similar to what happened to Kyle during the attempted bank robbery of 12 years ago when he was wearing the Seibert Anchor Cross and the robbers were about to lock him and three others in the bank vault, an act that if successful would surely have killed all four. So it is my contention as a Christian believer that all those souls on the Delta flight were spared a certain death by our possession of the Pelle Anchor Cross. Certainly this is not something we can prove, and it is something we do not understand, but it did happen. And then when we got back to Lexington and ran all the tests on the Pelle Anchor Cross we were able to determine that it was indeed made from the same gold as that of the Seibert Anchor Cross and that it was cast in the same mold. We thus established that the Pelle and Seibert Anchor Crosses are identical. They are indeed two of the six Savior's Crosses."

Randy then stepped away from the podium and to the front edge of the stage as he reached under his sweater, pulled out the Pelle Anchor Cross, and held it forward in his hand. He said, "Ladies and gentlemen, the Pelle Anchor Cross!"

There was an audible hush from the audience. Camera shutters could be heard clicking from all the reporters. Many in the crowd brought out cameras and began taking pictures. Deputy Kyle Potter and Trooper Ape Cornett immediately stood and walked beside Randy. A murmur then could be heard from the crowd as they began to talk with each other about the remarkable beauty of the Pelle Anchor Cross.

Mayor Knapp then walked to the podium and said, "Dr. Peters, we thank you so much for sharing the story and the Pelle Anchor Cross itself with us today. How remarkable it is that now two of these precious, priceless golden anchor crosses have found their way to Harlan County. This concludes all the presentations for today. I know you all feel as I do, that this has indeed been a historic day. Dr. Peters will continue for a while displaying the Pelle Anchor Cross for those that would like to get a good look or take pictures of it. Also, Anthony Beekins should be back shortly with the computer parts for display, and we'll place them here on the edge of the stage. Again, many thanks to the Governor, the Secretary, and the Senator for being with us, and thanks to each of you for all your interest and for being here today."

Applause broke out. The Senator, Governor, and Secretary walked over beside Randy to get a close look at the Pelle Anchor Cross.

Max moved his right hand slowly under his jacket and felt the string that was attached to the detonator. He closed his eyes, shouted Allahu Akbar, and pulled the string. Nothing happened. He pulled the string again. Nothing happened. He started jerking the string. Nothing happened. He then began beating on his jacket and pants. Nothing happened. His shout had not been heard because of the loud applause, but several on the stage noticed Max's strange behavior. He continued to beat on himself. He realized that the explosives were not going to detonate. At that moment he knew his only option to complete his mission was to use the gun that he carried stuck in his waistband. As he began to move his right hand to grab the pistol both his arms went completely limp. He tried to will his arms and hands to move, but they would not. Had he suffered a stroke? He felt okay, except his arms and hands were numb. He couldn't move them. They just hung at his side. Jake Keller had been watching Max and he stood and started walking toward him.

Randy then suddenly released the Pelle Anchor Cross from his hand and let it hang from its necklace about his neck. It had gotten very hot.

Just then there was an earsplitting explosion, and a large plume of smoke formed just to the Southwest. Windows rattled, one of the television camera platforms fell, people began to scream and run. Pandemonium broke loose. Two State Troopers in the crowd jumped on the stage and grabbed the politicians and started rushing them to their cars. Kyle and Ape stayed close to Randy to protect him and the Pelle Anchor Cross. Mayor Knapp grabbed the microphone at the podium and tried to appeal to the crowd to stay calm. But they didn't. Most just started running trying to get to their cars. They didn't know what the big explosion was, but they knew it was far from natural. In less than 5 minutes the crowd that had filled the Court House lawn and adjacent streets was gone. The remaining State Troopers joined with the Harlan City police to try and direct traffic. State Police post 10 had been called and had dispatched troopers to try and find the source of the explosion.

Jake Keller asked Max, "Are you having some kind of physical problem?"

Max replied, "I can't move my arms."

Jake said, "Hold on, I'll get help." He moved over to Kyle standing beside Randy and said, "Kyle, come over here and give me a hand. I think Mr. Robertson has had a stroke."

Kyle then told Ape to stay with Randy and he accompanied Jake over to take a look at Max.

"You having a problem?" Kyle asked Max.

"Can't move my arms," Max replied.

"Can you walk?" asked Kyle.

"Yes. I think so," Max replied.

"Come on, lets walk into the Sheriff's office, we'll get you some help," Kyle said.

Kyle and Jake stood one on each side of Max as they walked him off the stage and into the Sheriff's office. Kyle told him to have a seat at his desk and he would get Rosie to call for medical assistance. He quickly explained the situation to Rosie and asked her to call for an EMT. Kyle then told Max just to remain calm there at his desk and the EMTs would be there shortly. Kyle and Jake then left to return to the Court House lawn to try and find out what was going on.

Max knew that if the EMTs got him they would discover his faulty explosive suit and he would never be able to explain that. He had to get out of there, but he felt sure the deputy called Rosie would stop him if he tried to leave. At that point he noticed that his arms no longer felt numb. He tried to move his hands and they seemed to respond. If it was a stroke, it was a quick one. He seemed back to normal. He then reached for his gun, and pulled it from under his jacket. That was a mistake.

Preacher Puss had been taking in all the activity from her spot on the shelf above the door and Kyle's desk. Then she saw the man bring out a pistol. Out came the claws as she jumped.

Just when Max thought the strange stroke was over and he was going to be able to make a getaway, he felt a thud on the top of his head and the most excruciating pain ever. There was this furry tail swishing back and forth in his face as blood began to stream down his head. He dropped his gun and began to scream. He fell to the floor.

Rosie looked up just as Preacher Puss jumped. She saw the gun in the man's hand and she reached for her handcuffs. She ran around the counter and over to the man laying on the floor and put the handcuffs on him. Preacher Puss jumped back up to her shelf and laid back down contently. Rosie pulled Max to his feet and took him to the holding cell behind Bert's office. She locked him in the cell, returned to her office, and tried to call the Sheriff on his cell phone.

Chapter 28

I'll have 2 big macs, a large order of fries, and a chocolate milkshake," Fatso told the McDonalds employee. He hoped that she didn't notice that his hands were trembling as he paid for his meal. He didn't really have any idea how large that bomb was until he pressed that red button as he was nearing the Harlan by-pass. When he did the shock wave was strong enough that it rocked his car and the noise was as loud as he had ever heard. He understood then why Trigger didn't want to have anything to do with that going off in the large crowd of people. No doubt it would have killed hundreds.

After he regained his composure from the explosion Fatso drove South on the by-pass toward McDonalds for lunch. Two State Police cars passed him going back toward the explosion with their sirens screaming. He pulled in McDonalds for lunch, happy his errand was over.

•••

Just as soon as he heard the explosion Sheriff Sterling had jumped from the stage and run to his cruiser. He was ahead of all the panicking crowd, and he drove directly toward the large plume of smoke. He got on the by-pass for a short distance, and then across the Henry J. Giles memorial bridge to the Sunshine subdivision. He then drove only a couple of blocks and came to the site of the explosion. It was the old railroad yard. Apparently the bomb was sitting in an open area when it detonated. There was a huge hole in the earth at ground zero. The storage building that was located maybe 30 yards from where the bomb went off was completely gone .... totally leveled. People with homes located about a quarter of a mile away were out walking around their houses looking at the broken windows. Thankfully, as far as Bert could tell, no one had been injured by the blast.

Bert's cell phone rang. He answered and listened a moment then said, "Thanks Rosie, don't let that guy out for any reason. Keep him in the cell, I'll be back shortly."

•••

Tony had left the ceremony as planned. He had reached his car and left downtown Harlan. There was a good place to pull off the road on the outskirts of Harlan. He sat listening to the radio. The station was called WHLN. A few minutes passed and then he heard it. It was deafening. Then after the blast he looked back toward the town and saw the huge pillar of smoke. It looked to him a little too far to the West from downtown, but then he figured the wind had carried it. Ole Max had done the deed. Mission accomplished. He started up the car and headed down 119 toward Wallins.

Trigger was sitting at the cash register. He had his 38 revolver laying just under the counter where he could easily reach it. He saw Tony pull in the parking lot, and get out of his car carrying a duffel bag. He entered the store.

"Well, well Mr. Beekins," Trigger exclaimed. "Looks like my load of money has arrived."

"Where's Fatso," Tony asked.

"Had to run an errand," said Trigger. "I'm minding the store. Did everything go as planned?"

"It did," replied Tony. "Because I'm a man of my word, your $250,000 is in this bag. If anything had not gone as planned we would not be having this meeting. I know I could have just kept driving with your money, but in my business word gets around if you don't keep your contract." He placed the bag on the counter and turned to walk out.

"Hey, good to do business with you Tony. You have a good day!", Trigger said.

Tony did not respond. He walked to his car, got in, and drove off Southwest toward Pineville.

Trigger opened the bag. Sure enough, there appeared to be about $250,000 worth of cash .... all one hundred dollar bills. An enormous smile formed on his face. Just then he heard the doorbell tingle and looked up to see Fatso standing there.

"Hey Trigger, you know why elephants have trunks?"

"Cause they don't have glove compartments," replied Trigger. "I've heard your corny jokes a million times, Fatso. How did everything go with the errand?"

"Real good. No problems. Except I wasn't ready for the size of that bomb. I think it blew out every window within a mile. It shook my car, and I was just about on the by-pass at the time. That was really a big one," replied Fatso.

"How were things going at the ceremony?" asked Trigger.

Fatso answered, "They had a huge crowd. Everything seemed fine. All the speakers showed up, although Tony and Max were about five minutes late. Course I didn't get to hear the last two speakers, and missed getting to see that new golden cross thing. I left just like you told me to when Tony walked off the stage."

"Fatso, you've earned a bonus," Trigger replied. He then reached in the bag and pulled out a bundle of $100 bills. "I think there should be $10,000 there. And take the rest of the day off!"

Fatso's eyes got very large and he said, "Hey Trigger, you know what you get if you cross a mole with an elephant?"

Trigger pointed his finger toward the front door.

Fatso laughed, picked up the stack of money, turned and started walking toward the door. "When you cross a mole with an elephant you get big holes in your garden." Fatso chuckled and walked out the door.

Trigger walked around the counter and over to the door and placed the 'CLOSED' sign in its window. He thought, I'm going home and sleep till Monday.

•••

Bert arrived back at the Sheriff's office.

"Hey Rosie, sounds like you and ole Preacher Puss done caught us a criminal."

"I think you're right about that," Rosie said. "When he fell to the floor after Preacher Puss had about clawed him to death his wig fell off. Then I noticed that the inside of his suit coat was lined with pockets that had some kind of plastic covered material in them. It's kind of hard to imagine, but it sure looks like what we've got is one of those suicide bombers! Kyle was in here soon after I called you, and he got all excited that the stuff might blow up. He made the guy take all his clothes off and he said he was taking them to somewhere safe. He gave the guy some prisoner clothes to wear."

"Well, at least everything seems to be under control now. I don't have a clue what that explosion was all about, but fortunately no one was hurt. The insurance companies will be paying out a lot of broken window claims. Hopefully we'll be able to piece everything together before too long."

• • •

Anthony Beekins drove his rental car to the Knoxville, Tennessee airport and got a motel room for the evening. The next morning he planned to book a flight to Mexico City. After getting comfortable he turned on the television to check out the events in Harlan. The 10 o'clock news' lead story opened with shots of the Harlan County Courthouse and the reporter talked about the new computer parts plant that was to be built there and showed clips of the politicians' remarks and then his own face was prominently displayed on the screen as he gave his talk. What followed was a discussion about wine production in Harlan County and then a fellow displayed a golden anchor cross and talked about it for a while. Tony was getting very uncomfortable, he was starting to sweat. This was all going too smoothly. Max's bomb should have been the overwhelming story. Hundreds of people should have been killed. At that point in the newscast a very loud blast could be heard and the television camera shook violently, and then it turned from the Court House to look in another direction and there was a plume of smoke rising. The explosion did take place ..... just not at the Court House. All the color drained from Tony's face. He knew he was a dead man.

Chapter 29

Monday morning, October 12

The Sheriff and the Mayor sat at a table in Creech Cafe drinking coffee.

Mayor Knapp said, "Bert, talk about the good and the ugly. Saturday was full of both!"

Bert responded, "Yeah, it was. And the thing was, everything had gone so well right up to the very end. But looking back on it now I guess we were very fortunate indeed that no one really got hurt. If that suicide bomber had been able to detonate his explosive suit we would have had one of the worst imaginable situations. Hundreds of people would have been killed. As it turned out, about the only thing we really lost was that fake manufacturing plant. And I do have a really good feeling about Dom's Harlan

County wine being a giant catalyst for our economy. I think Jake Keller will work his magic and truly start something big."

"I think so too," replied Fred. "I'm just sorry the ceremony had to end on such a sour note. But as you said, no one was hurt, and for that we really need to be thankful. When did you find out that Max's suit was a dud?"

Bert said, "Kyle discovered soon after he took Max's suit that the pockets contained packages of sand rather than explosives. He took the suit to a remote wooded area and cut one of the packages in the pants. Sand poured out. Then he checked the other 6 packages and found the same thing. Someone must have switched the explosives for sand, and my guess is that the bomb that went off in the Sunshine subdivision contained Max's explosives."

"That is strange," Fred said. "I guess we'll never know anything more from Max."

"That's for sure, since he's now dead," replied Bert. "I felt bad that we couldn't arrest him, but the fact was we had absolutely nothing to charge him with other than possession of a firearm. And here in Harlan County carrying a gun is pretty common, some legal and most illegal. So we just confiscated the gun and let him go. I tried for a couple of hours to get him to talk about the suicide suit, but he really clammed up. I figured he'd stick around at least for a few days. He was staying with Trigger Green. But evidently when I released him he headed out of the county immediately. The Bell County Sheriff found him dead in his car not more than 30 minutes after his release here. He had just pulled his car off highway 119 after driving only about 15 miles. He must have had another gun in his car. So he did indeed wind up being a suicide bomber, just not the way he intended!"

"Praise the Lord, He had to be watching out for us," replied Fred.

"Well, I think we actually have evidence of that," said Bert. "As best I can piece it together, when he failed to detonate his suit he decided to use his handgun to shoot someone, and my guess is that his target was the Senator because Tony had requested that Senator McDonald announce his new plant. At that time the Senator was standing with Randy looking at the Pelle Anchor Cross. We know the Cross got so hot that Randy had to drop it and let it hang from its necklace, and I think the reason for that was that Max was preparing to fire a shot at the Senator, but Randy was likely in the line of sight. As a Christian believer, I think the Lord brought about Max's stroke-like condition that prevented him from being able to hold and fire the gun. No way I can prove what I just said, but to me it makes the most sense."

"I agree 100 percent with you," the Mayor responded. "I think what you said is certainly the explanation for Max's short-term stroke. I guess the big mystery is how and why his suicide suit explosives got switched. You got any ideas on that?"

"Actually, I do," Bert replied. "I think the answer is known by Trigger Green. Max was staying with Trigger, and I think something happened for some reason to cause Trigger or someone he hired to do the switch. Problem is, I can't prove it. But I do plan to pay him a visit to see what he'll say."

Fred replied, "Makes sense. And do you think we'll ever know what happened to Tony Beekins? Apparently when he left the stage at the ceremony he took off to parts unknown. I understand he stuck the Holiday Inn Express with a big bill .... when they tried to run his credit card they found it was stolen. I'm sure his real name likely wasn't Anthony Beekins."

"I'm sure you're right there," answered Bert. "Both he and Max had their tracks covered pretty good. But since there was an apparent attempt to kill the politicians the FBI is now involved so maybe they'll turn up something on Tony."

"We'll keep our fingers crossed," replied the Mayor.

Bert then said, "I do think we did the right thing to keep the attempted suicide bombing from the media. Eventually it'll leak out that Max was wearing that suit, but for the time being the large explosion and the revelation that AB Enterprises was phony are enough negatives to keep them busy. I've told all my staff to keep everything under wraps about the suicide suit."

Fred replied, "Good. I did think the press conference yesterday went well. It was obvious that they wanted more answers about the explosion and about the phony AB Enterprises, but we truthfully told them what we knew, which was very little. We just hedged on the suicide bomber thing. And since they didn't know about it we didn't have to answer any questions. My gut feeling is that before too long we'll be able to find the answers. When we do we can then release them. I was thankful that all the television coverage Saturday evening and yesterday, and the newspaper articles yesterday put a good spin on the Pelle wine development. And they all certainly did cover the Pelle Anchor Cross story well also. The photographs of it were spectacular, both on TV and in the newspapers."

"Yeah, I think for the time being everything is good. We'll continue to very aggressively pursue an explanation for both the explosion and the suicide suit explosives switch, and to trying to track down Anthony Beekins. I think Rosie is really looking forward to our being able to release everything on the suicide bomber so that she can tell the story about Preacher Puss's capturing him! When that news gets out ole Preacher Puss will again reign supreme in the Sheriff's Office!" said Bert.

The mayor replied with a chuckle, "That cat's earned a lifetime supply of Whisker Lickins and a 5 Star retirement plan."

"I'm just hoping he doesn't decide to run for Sheriff," Bert responded.

•••

Randy and Dom had driven back to Lexington after the press conference on Sunday. After a good night's rest the two were sitting in Randy's kitchen having morning coffee and toast.

Randy said, "Dom, I guess it would be safe to say that the ceremony wound up with a bang!"

"Nobody could argue with that," replied Dom. "It is sad the explosion happened. And I still can't make sense out of all that suicide bomber thing. I'm just glad the press didn't get wind of it. When they do it'll raise a big stink."

Randy replied, "Let's just hope Bert can come up with a good explanation that will satisfy everyone. And I do think he will .... he just needs a little time. But on the positive side, Pelle's Harlan County grape and wine operation is off and running, and it certainly seemed that your announcement was extremely well received."

"I felt real good about it," Dom replied. "I think the Kellers will develop the business in a grand fashion, and I look forward to coming back frequently to work with them. Also, I've decided that the Pelle Anchor Cross should remain here in Lexington in your Center along with the Seibert Anchor Cross. I've talked with Father Gi about it, and we're both in agreement. I'll make a little contribution to your Center that should enable you to properly display it beside the Seibert Anchor Cross".

"Thank you my friend," Randy said. "I'll make certain it get's the very utmost of attention and care. It will be a superb addition to the Center."

"It has certainly been a most interesting trip," said Dom. "There's seldom been a dull moment! I'll be heading back to Prato tomorrow. Without the Pelle Anchor Cross I'll just have to keep my fingers crossed that the cockpit crew doesn't suffer simultaneous heart attacks! Your hospitality has just been super. Thank you so much for everything."

"Dom the pleasure was certainly all mine. I've enjoyed so very much meeting and getting to know you, and I'll look forward greatly to being in touch with you and to your frequent visits back to Lexington and Harlan."

The two then drove to the University and took care of business for the day in preparation for Dom's departure tomorrow.

Chapter 30

One week later, October 19th

S heriff J. Bert Sterling was sitting in his office when Rosie called on the intercom to tell him he had a call on line 1 from a Mr. Collins with the FBI.

"I'll take it," Bert replied. "Sheriff Sterling speaking."

On the other end of the line Mr. Collins replied, "Sheriff, my name is Roy Collins. I'm a special agent with the FBI in Miami. I'm calling to discuss with you what we have learned about the person called Mr. Anthony Beekins and his involvement in the events there in Harlan on October 10th."

"Great. I sure hope you've been able to find some answers," replied Bert.

Mr. Collins continued, "Well, we have. First of all,

just as soon as you reported the attempt to kill the Senator and that Mr. Beekins was a missing person of interest, we phoned the Holiday Inn Express and ordered them to seal his room. We had a forensics team there within hours, and they were able to lift fingerprints from a glass in his room. From these we identified him as Carlos Santiago, a Mexican national with quite a rap sheet. Then we got lucky when he used his real name when purchasing a plane ticket at Knoxville, Tennessee for Mexico City. As soon as his name was given to purchase the ticket we had him. We then had one of our agents in Mexico City meet the plane and follow him to his home. We then set up a stake-out since we didn't have enough evidence for an arrest or even for a warrant to search his home. After 2 days we again got lucky. Our people on stake-out noticed a car parked nearby that looked suspicious. When Santiago walked out of his home headed for his car the person in the suspicious car rolled down his window and produced a rifle. Our stake-out team got to the person before he could fire and cuffed him. They then stopped Santiago as he was pulling out of his driveway and forced him, along with the would-be assassin, to accompany them back to the motel where they were staying. The two were placed in handcuffs in separate rooms, and then our people started to interrogate the would-be assassin. They found his passport, and it established that he was from the Sudan. He would not offer other explanation about his actions. We then started to interrogate Santiago. We told him that a hit- man from the Sudan had just made an attempt to kill him. We also told him that we knew all about his attempted bombing in Harlan from interrogating Max Robertson. This was a bit of a fabrication, but we thought it might work since he didn't likely know that Robertson was dead. It did work. I think when I said that the hit-man was from the Sudan it really scared him. He wanted to deal. I told him we would offer him safety in our protection program and immunity from prosecution if he would cooperate with us. He took it. He told us that he was hired by an agent from the Sudan to make all arrangements required for a suicide bomber to be able to kill Senator McDonald. Max Robertson was that bomber."

"Wow," Bert replied. "So now we know for sure that Max Robertson intended to kill the Senator and anyone else impacted by the bomb, and we know that Carlos Santiago, aka Anthony Beekins, was hired by a Sudanese agent to facilitate the whole thing. But were you able to find out why they wanted to kill the Senator?"

Mr. Collins continued, "Yes, we were. From the fingerprints of Max Robertson we were able to establish that his real name was Muhammad Ahmad. He worked previously as a researcher on the staff of Senator McDonald in Washington. Ahmad was a native of the Sudan. As it turns out, McDonald's staff had prepared a report recommending that the U.S. discontinue foreign aid to the Sudan because much of it was being passed to the Sudan Peoples Liberation Army, the SPLA, an extreme terrorist group. Ahmad leaked this information back to the Sudanese government. So in order to keep the Senator from moving this recommendation forward the Sudanese government decided that Ahmad would please Allah by being a suicide bomber to eliminate the Senator."

"Remarkable," Bert said. "So that pretty much clears up everything except the explosion and why the explosives in the suit were switched and who switched them."

"Yeah. Can't help you there," Mr. Collins replied. "We can just be thankful they were. Otherwise we'd be dealing with a huge mass murder."

Bert asked, "Mr. Collins, did your people question Trigger Green?"

Collins replied, "Oh yes indeed. We spent a few hours with him. We knew, of course, that Ahmad was staying with Green, and that Santiago had been working closely with him in setting up the phony company as an alibi for getting Ahmad close enough to the Senator to be able to kill him. But Green pretty much clammed up and just claimed that he was hoodwinked by the two and honestly thought they intended to develop the proposed manufacturing plant. And he said he had been paid a handsome amount to lease his property to them. We knew that wasn't true, but we couldn't prove it."

"Mr. Collins I thank you and the Bureau sincerely for all this information. It certainly clears up a lot of things. I have been postponing a visit with Mr. Green until I heard from you. I think the time has now arrived for that visit," replied the Sheriff.

•••

The door bell jingled.

"Well, well, well. If it isn't the Sheriff of Harlan County," Fatso proclaimed.

"Fatso, I need to talk with you and Trigger ..... now," Bert replied.

"Well, business is a little slow, I guess we could go in his office and chat. You happened to catch him in," Fatso replied as he pressed the button to open the lock on Trigger's door and walked out from behind the counter and accompanied the Sheriff into Trigger's office.

Trigger was already standing when the two entered his office. He had been watching them on the closed circuit television.

Trigger said, "Sheriff Sterling, what a pleasure to have you visit me in my humble establishment. Please have a seat. Can I get you coffee?"

"No thanks," Bert replied. "I just need to talk with the two of you."

"Oh, and what might we need to talk about?" replied Trigger.

"I think you can guess. Let's quit pussyfooting around. I'm here to try and get some answers," said Bert.

"I'm all ears," Trigger replied.

Bert began, "I'm not going to beat around the bush with you two. I think you know far better than I do what really happened on October 10th. But I do know a few things that you likely don't know. Police things that haven't been made public. I'm going to tell them to you, and I do ask that you keep them to yourselves. Number one, our friend Max Robertson was a terrorist from Sudan. His real name was Muhammad Ahmad. He had worked on the staff of Senator McDonald and had discovered that the Senator was getting ready to release a recommendation to eliminate foreign aid to the Sudan because it was being funneled to a terrorist group there. The Sudanese government then sent him to Harlan in a plot to kill the Senator. After his failed suicide bombing he killed himself over in Bell County. While we had him in custody we were not able to get any information from him. Number two, Anthony Beekins is an international assassin and thug employed by anyone with enough money to get his services. The Sudanese government employed him to take care of all the planning to get Ahmad close enough to the Senator to kill him. After the ceremony on October 10th he flew to Mexico City His real name is Carlos Santiago. The FBI captured him when an assassin from the Sudanese government attempted to shoot him. They were successful in talking him into a witness protection program in exchange for his telling them who was behind the attempted suicide bombing of Senator McDonald."

Bert then stopped talking and just stared at Trigger and Fatso for about a minute.

Then Bert continued, "So now you know what happened to those two. One's dead, and the other is put away in a closely controlled witness protection program. You'll never see them again. Two big questions remain unanswered. What was the explosion all about, and who switched the explosives out of the suicide suit. I think you two might be able to help me here."

Trigger spoke up, "Well, Sheriff, a person has to be real careful when he's talking to the law. You know what I mean?"

Bert replied, "Trigger, let me assure you that if you confirm what I think happened you will not be in trouble."

"That's a start," said Trigger. "Exactly what do you think happened?"

Bert continued, "I think you switched the explosives on Ahmad. He was staying at your house and you therefore had access to the suit. The only reason I can come up with for your doing that was that you got in a lot deeper than you originally bargained for. I think you did not want to see hundreds of people murdered. And I think the explosion was carried out by Fatso to somehow enable you to deceive Santiago into thinking that the plot had been successful. I know the Mayor saw Fatso leave the ceremony about the same time that Santiago left. My guess is that Fatso took the bomb to the Sunshine subdivision and triggered it. If my thinking is correct, you two are actually responsible for saving the lives of hundreds of people. The public will never know this, but if that's true then I'm here to thank you."

Trigger looked at Fatso. Fatso looked back at Trigger. Then the two of them simultaneously looked directly at Bert and started to smile. They then both started to nod their heads in agreement. Words were not necessary.

Bert stood, patted Fatso on the shoulder and shook hands with Trigger. He then turned and started to walk out.

Fatso said, "Hey Sheriff, you know how you stop an elephant from smelling?"

Bert walked on through the door and closed it behind him.

"You stop an elephant from smelling by tying a knot in his trunk," Fatso said to the closed door.